"Jordan?"

If Layla Grandin said that name one more time, he was liable to snap. Joshua's blood boiled in his veins. He was frustrated with the dumb twin switch and desperately attracted to the woman he had taken on a faux date this evening.

"Layla?" He said her name gruffly, wishing he could blurt out the truth. But his original plan was best. Let this "Jordan" relationship expire, and then Joshua could swoop in and play cleanup.

"Yes?" Her smile was tentative now. Perhaps the tone of his voice had spooked her. It was hard for a guy to play it cool when every cell in his body wanted the woman sitting two feet away.

"Will you have dinner with me tomorrow night?"

Where did that come from? No way was he going to let "Jordan" go out with Layla again.

* * *

Staking a Claim by Janice Maynard is part of the Texas Cattleman's Club: Ranchers and Rivals series.

Dear Reader,

It's always fun to go back to Royal, Texas, and see what new drama is looming on the horizon. This time, we are looking at family secrets.

Does your family have some? I suppose they can be good or bad. As an adult, I discovered that my great-aunt (my grandmother's sister) had a six-month marriage years ago that was either dissolved or ended in divorce. By the time I heard this secret, all the people who could have enlightened me were gone.

As a kid, I assumed that my aunt was a typical "old maid" who had never married. Isn't it awful that we used to hear that term all the time? Children rarely understand the complexities of adulthood. I hope my aunt had a good life despite what must have been a terribly difficult period.

The good thing about a fictional family is that we can enjoy their problems without stress. I hope you enjoy getting to know the Grandins. There are a bunch of them, and they each have their share of stubborn traits.

Thanks for loving and reading romance!

Fondly,

Janice Maynard

JANICE MAYNARD

STAKING A CLAIM

HARLEQUIN
DESIRE

Special thanks and acknowledgment are given to
Janice Maynard for her contribution to the
Texas Cattleman's Club: Ranchers and Rivals miniseries.

Recycling programs
for this product may
not exist in your area.

ISBN-13: 978-1-335-73558-4

Staking a Claim

Harlequin Enterprises ULC
22 Adelaide St. West, 41st Floor
Toronto, Ontario M5H 4E3, Canada
www.Harlequin.com

Printed in U.S.A.

USA TODAY bestselling author **Janice Maynard** loved books and writing even as a child. After multiple rejections, she finally sold her first manuscript! Since then, she has written more than sixty books and novellas. Janice lives in Tennessee with her husband, Charles. They love hiking, traveling and family time.

You can connect with Janice at
www.janicemaynard.com,
www.Twitter.com/janicemaynard,
www.Facebook.com/janicemaynardauthor,
www.Facebook.com/janicesmaynard and
www.Instagram.com/therealjanicemaynard.

Books by Janice Maynard

Harlequin Desire

Southern Secrets

Blame It On Christmas
A Contract Seduction
Bombshell for the Black Sheep

The Men of Stone River

After Hours Seduction
Upstairs Downstairs Temptation
Secrets of a Playboy

Texas Cattleman's Club: Ranchers and Rivals

Staking a Claim

Visit her Author Profile page at Harlequin.com,
or janicemaynard.com, for more titles.

You can also find Janice Maynard on Facebook,
along with other Harlequin Desire authors,
at Facebook.com/harlequindesireauthors!

For Anastasia, Ainsley, Allie, Levi and Hattie.
You are the best of all of us!
I hope you continue to stay as close
as you are now...

One

Layla Grandin hated funerals. It was bad enough to sit through somber affairs with friends who had lost family members. But today was worse. Today was personal.

Victor Grandin Sr., Layla's beloved grandfather, had been laid to rest.

It wasn't a tragedy in the truest sense of the word. Victor was ninety-three years old when he died. He lived an amazing, fulfilling life. And in the end, he was luckier than most. He literally died with his boots on after suffering a heart attack while on horseback.

There were worse ways to go. But that didn't make Layla's grief any less.

After the well-attended funeral in town, many of Royal's finest citizens had made the trek out to the Grandin ranch to pay their respects. Layla eyed the large gathering with a cynical gaze. The Grandin family was wealthy. Even folks with the best of intentions couldn't help sniffing around when money and inheritance were on the menu. That was the burden of financial privilege. You never knew if people really liked you or if they just wanted something they thought you could give them.

For that very reason, Layla had been lingering in the corner of the room, content to play voyeur. Her newly widowed grandmother Miriam looked frail and distraught, as was to be expected. Layla's father was relishing the role of genial host, embracing his chance to shine now that his larger-than-life parent was out of the picture.

Layla wished with all her heart that her own father cared for her as much as her gruff but loving grandfather had. Unfortunately, Victor Junior was not particularly interested in his female offspring. He was too focused on his only son, Victor the third, better known as Vic. Her father was grooming Vic to take over one day, despite the fact that Layla's older sister, Chelsea, was first in line, followed by Layla.

Chelsea crossed the room in Layla's direction, looking disgruntled. "I am so over this," she said. "I don't think anyone here really cares about Grandfather at all. Some of them probably haven't even met him."

Layla grimaced. "I know what you mean. But at least Vic and Morgan are genuinely upset. Grandy loved all his grandkids."

"You most of all," Chelsea said. "You were the only one who could get away with that nickname."

Layla flushed. She hadn't realized anyone else noticed. As the middle of three girls, and with Vic their father's clear favorite, Layla often felt lost in the crowd.

Suddenly, Layla realized her father was deep in conversation with a man she recognized. She lowered her voice and leaned toward Chelsea. "Why is Daddy cozied up to Bertram Banks? Oh, crap! Why are they looking at me?"

"Who knows? Let's go find out." Chelsea, always the proactive one, took Layla's elbow and steered her across the room. Layla would have much preferred hiding out in the kitchen, but the two men obviously saw them approaching.

When they were in earshot, Layla and Chelsea's dad gave them a big smile. For such a sober day, it might have been a bit too big, in Layla's estimation.

"Here are my two oldest," he said, giving Bertram a wink. "Take your pick."

Chelsea raised an eyebrow. "That sounds a little weird, Dad."

Bertram chuckled. "He didn't mean anything by it."

Layla distrusted the two men's good humor. Both of them were known to manipulate people when the occasion demanded it. Layla had known the Banks family forever. As a kid, she had been a tomboy, running wild and riding horses and dirt bikes with Bertram's twin sons, Jordan and Joshua.

Back then, she was lean and coltish, not at all interested in girly pursuits. She could take whatever the Banks boys dished out. As she grew older, though, she'd developed a terrible crush on Jordan. It was embarrassing to think about now.

"What's going on?" Layla asked.

For once, Chelsea was silent.

Bertram smiled at Layla. This time it seemed genuine. "I have tickets to see Parker Brett in concert tomorrow night."

It was Layla's turn to raise an eyebrow. "Congratulations. I've heard those were impossible to get."

Bertram puffed out his chest. "I know a guy," he said, chuckling. "But the thing is, I've had a conflict arise. Jordan has offered to take you, Layla, you know—to cheer you up. We all know how much you loved your grandfather."

Layla was aghast. Chelsea bit her lip, clearly trying hard not to laugh. She knew all about Layla's fruitless crush.

To be honest, Layla highly doubted that Jordan had volunteered to do anything of the sort. She wasn't even sure he liked country music. "That's sweet of you," she said. "But I don't think I'll feel like going out. This has been an emotional week."

Her father jumped in. "It will do you good, Layla. Everyone knows you've had a crush on Jordan forever."

A split second of stunned silence reverberated between the uncomfortable foursome. *Did he just say that? Oh, yes he did!* Layla felt her face get hot. *Recover, Layla. Quickly! Think!* "When I was a kid, Dad. I've moved on," Layla mumbled.

Chelsea tried to help. "Good grief, Daddy. Layla's had a million boyfriends since then. Even a fiancé." She stopped short, clearly appalled. "Sorry, sis."

Layla forced a smile. Her doomed engagement two years ago was a sore spot, more because it reeked of failure than anything else. "No worries." She faced the duo of late-fifties males. "I'm sure Jordan can find his own date for the concert."

Bertram's expression was bland, suspiciously innocent. "You're it, kiddo. He'll text you the details later tonight."

Layla glanced around the room. "He's not here?"

"He went to the funeral, but he had another commitment this afternoon."

Victor beamed. "So, it's settled. If you two ladies will excuse us, Bertram and I are going to mingle."

When the two men wandered away, Layla groaned. "You have to be kidding me. Why didn't you say something? I needed help."

Chelsea cocked her head, her sisterly smile teasing. "Well, he wasn't wrong. You *have* always had a thing for Jordan Banks. What could it hurt to get out of the house? With you swearing off men after your engagement ended and now Grandfather dying, I think it would do you good. It's just a concert."

Layla couldn't disagree with the logic. "Fine," she said. "But I hope this doesn't put Jordan in a weird spot. I'll have to make sure he knows I'm not pining for him."

"I'm sure he doesn't think that." Chelsea grinned.

Layla had been too tense and upset to eat lunch before the funeral. Now she was starving. Her mother had made arrangements for catered hors d'oeuvres to serve the dozens of guests who showed up for the reception. Judging by the crowd, it might ultimately prove to be two hundred or two fifty. But her mother, Bethany, was an experienced hostess. No one would run out of food.

"Let's get something to eat," Layla said to Chelsea.

"Good idea."

The two sisters filled their plates and retreated to a sunny alcove just off the large living room. Some people might be taken aback by the luxurious, enormous house, but to Layla and Chelsea it was simply home.

From their comfortable seats, they enjoyed the sunshine and the food. Chelsea sighed. "I can't believe it's only four days till May. Summer will be here soon."

Layla's composure wobbled. "Grandy loved the long days and even the heat. Not to mention watermelon and fresh corn. It won't be the same this year." She scanned the crowd. "I guess we should have asked Morgan to join us." Chelsea was thirty-five, Layla thirty-two. Morgan, their baby sister, was still in her twenties.

"She's hanging out with Vic," Chelsea said, stabbing a fat shrimp with her fork. "Did I tell you she sided with Vic over me yesterday? Again."

Vic was third in line, but first in their father's heart and plans.

Chelsea continued, "Every damn time she takes Vic's side. Just once I'd like her to take mine. Still, it's not their fault Daddy thinks I can't handle the ranch eventually. It makes me so angry. I love this ranch as much as anybody. It ought to be me. Or you and me together."

"Well, it won't, so you might as well get used to the idea. Besides, if genetics are any clue, Daddy will live another thirty years. You and I might as well forget about this ranch and find something else to keep us busy."

"True," Chelsea said glumly.

"Look at Mr. Lattimore," Layla said. "He must be grieving terribly, but he's as dignified as ever." Augustus was ninety-six. His wife, Hazel, was at his side speaking to him in a low voice. As a Black family in Royal, Texas, the Lattimores hadn't always had it easy, but they were equally as influential as the Grandins. The only difference was, their patriarch, Augustus, had been forced to give up the reins several years ago because of his struggles with memory issues.

"He and Grandfather were so very close. I wonder

if he understands that Grandfather is gone. They've been friends for decades." Chelsea's comment was wistful.

"His memory comes in flashes, I think. You've seen people like that." The two families were so close the Lattimore kids probably felt sad about losing Grandpa Victor even if he wasn't their blood kin. It would be hard to see the oldest generation begin to pass on, especially since they adored their own grandfather.

Chelsea put her plate on a side table and grimaced. "I hate funerals," she said.

Layla burst out laughing.

Her sister gaped. "Did I say something funny?"

"Not particularly," Layla said, still chuckling. "But I've been thinking the same thing all day. When it's my time to go, just put me in the ground and plant a tree. I don't need people kicking the dirt and fighting over my estate."

"Always assuming you have one."

"Touché." Chelsea's joking comment gave Layla something to ponder. After college, she had spent the last decade pouring her energies into this place. She assisted her mother with frequent entertaining. She helped train horses. And though her father was sometimes dismissive of her expertise, she used her business degree to make sure the family enterprise was solid.

Her grandfather had been proud of her ideas and her knack for understanding the ranching business.

Unfortunately, he was too old-school to ever think a woman could be in charge of anything that didn't involve cooking, cleaning or changing diapers. A woman's place was in the home.

No matter that he had been affectionate and supportive of Layla's thoughts and dreams, he had been forged in the patriarchal environs of Maverick County, and he agreed with his son. The only grandson, Vic, should be next in line to run things when it was Victor Junior's time to hang up his spurs.

Layla was at a crossroads. Her personal life was nonexistent. If Vic was going to be heir to the Grandin ranch, she might as well make a plan for the future. Many of her friends were married and had kids by now. Layla didn't feel any rush.

Her ex-fiancé, Richard, hadn't been too excited about the prospect of starting a family. That should have been a red flag. But Layla had taken his words at face value. He'd said he was concentrating on his career.

Unfortunately, the thing he'd been concentrating on was screwing as many women as possible in the shortest amount of time. The only reason he'd given Layla a ring was that he saw the benefit in allying himself with the Grandin empire.

For Layla, the entire experience had shaken her confidence. How could she trust her own judgment when she had been so wrong about Richard?

Gradually, the crowd thinned. She and Chelsea split up to mingle, to thank people for coming and to say goodbyes. The food tables were demolished. The furniture was askew. By all accounts, the funeral reception was a success. Hazel and Augustus Lattimore were just now being escorted home. Layla's grandmother Miriam looked shaky and exhausted as she headed for her suite.

Fortunately for Layla, Bertram Banks had disappeared half an hour ago. She definitely didn't want to talk to him again. She was already planning how to ditch the concert arrangements.

She had nothing against country music. Jordan would be a fun companion. But she was emotionally wrung out. In some ways, she had never completely processed the trauma from two years ago, and now this, losing her grandfather.

As the room emptied, only the Grandins and Lattimores remained, parents and kids, though the term *kids* was a misnomer. Even Caitlyn, the youngest, was twenty-five. The reception had been advertised as a drop-in from two until five. Now it was almost six.

Layla was about to make her excuses and head to her bedroom when her mother went to answer the doorbell and came back flanked by a uniformed person holding a legal-size envelope.

Oddly, the room fell silent. The young courier looked nervous. "I have a delivery addressed to The Heirs of Victor Grandin Sr.," he said.

Layla's father stepped forward. "That's me. Where do I sign?"

Ben Lattimore, her father's best friend, joined him. "What's up? Kind of late in the day for any kind of official delivery."

Victor nodded absently, breaking the seal on the envelope and extracting the contents. After a moment, he paled. "Someone is pursuing the oil rights to both of our ranches."

"Somebody who?" Chelsea asked, trying to read over Victor's shoulder.

He scanned farther. "Heath Thurston."

Ben frowned. "Why didn't I get a copy?"

"Maybe you did at your house." Victor glared at the document. "It's in incredibly poor taste to deliver this today."

"The timing could be a coincidence." Ben Lattimore was visibly worried. "If this is legit, our properties are in trouble. We're cattle ranchers, damn it. Having somebody search for oil would destroy much of what we've built."

Vic stepped to his father's shoulder. "I thought we didn't have any oil, right? So this is probably all a hoax," he said. "Don't worry about it, Dad. At least not until we investigate."

"That's the ticket," Victor said. "I know a PI—Jonas Shaw." His gaze narrowed. "But I'll start with my mother first."

Layla shook her head. "No, Daddy. She's grief-stricken and so frail right now. We should only involve her if it's absolutely necessary." It was obvious that her father didn't like being opposed. But he nodded tersely.

"I suppose," he said grudgingly. "But *you*…" He pointed at his brother. "I'm going to need cooperation from you, Daniel."

"I'm flying back to Paris tomorrow."

"Not anymore. No one leaves Royal until we meet with our lawyer."

Layla could tell Daniel wanted to argue. But he settled for a muttered protest. "This whole thing smells fishy," he said.

Conversation swelled as the two families broke up into small groups and began to process the bizarre information. Layla was surprised that Heath Thurston would pursue something like this. From what she knew of him, he was an honorable man. But if he and his brother thought they were entitled to the oil rights, maybe they were taking the only logical step.

Still, it was very suspicious that Thurston was claiming oil rights under *both* ranches. What possible claim could he have?

Layla spotted Alexa Lattimore gathering up her purse and light jacket, preparing to leave. Layla had talked to her earlier in the day, but only briefly. "Don't rush off, Alexa. I miss you." The eldest Lattimore daughter hadn't lived in Royal since finishing college.

"I've missed you, too, Layla. I was sorry to hear about your engagement. I wish I could have come home to give you moral support, but things were crazy at work."

Layla sighed. "It's no fun being the subject of Royal's grapevine. I don't think Richard broke my heart, but he definitely dented my pride." She tugged her friend to a nearby sofa. "I wanted to ask you something."

Alexa sat down with a wary expression. "Oh?"

"I was hoping you might think about coming home for a longer visit. I think Caitlyn would love having you around, and besides, it looks like your lawyer skills may be in demand. For both our families."

Alexa chewed her lip, not quite meeting Layla's gaze. "I don't know, Layla. I wanted to pay my respects at your grandfather's funeral, but this was just a quick jaunt. Miami is home now. There's no real place for me in Royal."

"If I know you, Ms. Workaholic, you probably have a million vacation days banked. At least think about it."

"I will," Alexa said.

Even hearing the words, Layla wasn't sure Alexa was telling the truth. Alexa had kept her distance from Royal and didn't seem eager to get involved with an ongoing crisis.

At last, Layla was free to escape to her bedroom and recover from this long, painful day. She stripped off her funeral dress and took a quick shower. After that, she donned comfy black yoga pants and a chunky teal sweater.

When she curled up in her chaise lounge by the window, the tears flowed. She'd been holding them in check all day. Now she sobbed in earnest. She would never see Grandy again, never hear the comfortable rumble of his voice. She had loved him deeply, but perhaps she had never realized just how big a void he filled in her life.

With Grandy gone, she felt adrift.

In the end, she had to wash her face and reapply mascara. The family would be gathering for dinner at seven thirty. It was the Grandin way, and old traditions were hard to break.

Just before she went downstairs at a quarter after, she glanced at her phone. All her family and friends had been at the house today, so there was no real reason to think she might have a text.

But Bertram had said Jordan would text her tonight.

It was dumb to feel hurt and uncertain. She knew Bertram. He was probably, even now, pressuring his son to take Layla to the concert. It was so embarrassing. Bertram would like nothing more than to have one of his sons marry a Grandin daughter. He wasn't picky. He would keep trying if this didn't work out.

The concert was a day away. If Layla hadn't heard from Jordan in the next couple of hours, she was done with this shotgun-date situation. She might have a long-standing crush on Jordan, but honestly, it was more like the feelings she'd had for a rock star or a movie idol growing up.

Doodling her name and Jordan's in hearts and flowers had been something fun. A fantasy to entertain herself. By the time she was an engaged woman, she had known her feelings for Jordan were mostly superficial. Still, the idea of a night on the town wasn't *so* terrible.

Layla would be the envy of every single woman in Royal, Texas.

What could it hurt to enjoy herself? She had been far too serious for far too long. She had let her mistakes and missteps make her afraid to live life.

Jordan Banks wasn't her soul mate. But he was handsome and temporarily available. And from what she remembered of him, he knew how to have fun.

That was what Layla needed…fun. This one date might not be a long-term solution to her solitary state, but it was a start. She needed to open herself up to possibilities…to surprises. No telling what might happen.

Two

Joshua Banks felt more unsettled than at any point in his life. He'd come home to Royal hoping for a signpost pointing his feet to a next step. It was time for a change. He was determined to seize control of his destiny, no matter how grandiose that sounded. Now, after an afternoon of driving aimlessly around Maverick County, his life in Dallas seemed a million miles away. Surely he had made the right choice.

Time would tell. For now, he was checked into a hotel and about to have dinner with his twin brother. Jordan would likely press for Joshua to stay at the ranch. It was the home where both men had grown up, after all. But Joshua needed some personal space…some time to sort out his feelings about his divorce and the really good job he had abandoned amidst a surge of hope about starting over in his hometown.

Thirty minutes later, he pulled up in front of a familiar steakhouse. The ambience was laid-back, the drinks cold and the music not so loud that he and Jordan couldn't talk comfortably. When Joshua stepped out of his car, he saw his brother execute the same maneuver a few spaces away.

That was nothing new. As identical twins, they'd always had the internal radar thing between them. To be honest, though, the sibling connection had weakened during the years Joshua had lived in Dallas.

His brother hugged him. "Man, it's good to see you, Josh."

Joshua was caught off guard by a wave of emotion. "Same here."

Inside, the hostess found them a table in a corner, handed over menus and left them alone. To his dismay, Joshua realized that he felt awkward. Maybe that's what happened when you hid too many secrets.

After they ordered drinks and dinner, Jordan rocked his chair back on two legs. "Damn, bro. You look good. Why do I have the beginnings of a beer gut, but you don't?"

Joshua chuckled. "It's called being a workaholic. No time for goofing off."

"If you say so." Jordan snagged an onion ring from their appetizer sampler and popped it in his mouth. "You know I don't beat around the bush. Why is this dinner just you and me? Why wasn't Dad invited?"

Joshua winced and rubbed the back of his neck. "Actually," he said slowly, "I'll have plenty of time to catch up with Dad. I've left Dallas for good."

The chair hit the ground. Jordan stared. "No shit? What about your job?"

"I resigned." Joshua could barely say the words out loud. What kind of person gave up a high-six-figure job with cushy perks? Especially with no definite plan in sight?

Jordan frowned. "I thought you loved your job."

"I did. Mostly. But I've been missing Royal. Dumb, huh? I always wanted to head for the big city, and now I find myself envying you."

"Dad will take you back at the ranch in a hot second."

"You think?"

"He never wanted you to leave in the beginning."

Joshua sighed. "If I'm hoping to come back into the fold, I'll have to eat a lot of crow and listen to a few dozen *I told you so*'s. He never liked Becky in the first place."

Turns out, the old man had been right about a lot of things. Becky had, indeed, been more interested in the Banks family money than in Joshua, himself. When they settled in Dallas after the wedding, the cracks in the relationship began to show.

Joshua had unfortunately been blinded by great sex and a master manipulator. He was partly to blame. He had convinced himself he was in love with Becky. It was why he had married her.

He'd never been more wrong.

The server dropped off two steaming plates. Jordan cut into his steak. "So where do things stand between you and the former Mrs. Banks?"

"Luckily I haven't seen her. When the divorce was final in February, as you know, she got the house in the settlement. I moved into an apartment and never looked back."

He and Becky had separated two years ago. The marriage had been over at least a year before that. It was a sad, sucky situation and one that had taught him valuable lessons. He was glad Jordan had been there whenever Josh needed him.

Joshua stabbed a bite of perfectly cooked rib eye. "And now here I am. What have you been up to… besides working your ass off at the ranch?"

"Well, today, it was a funeral. Victor Grandin died."

"I didn't even know he was still around. He had to be older than dirt."

"Ninety-three. The grandkids were broken up about it. And his wife, of course. But I don't think Victor Junior was too upset. He's been wanting to run that ranch on his own terms for a long time. The old man never would give up the reins."

"Wow." Joshua shook his head slowly, remembering the good times he had spent there. "I guess there will be some changes on the way."

"No doubt." Jordan finished his beer and grinned. It was a sly smile, one Joshua recognized all too well. His brother was up to something. "I need a favor, Josh. And in exchange, I'll run interference with Dad for you. Soften him up. Hint that you'd like to be back in the thick of things full-time."

"That's an awfully generous gesture. What would I have to do in return?" Joshua was on his guard. Jordan was a great guy, but he was slippery.

"Hardly anything at all. Take a beautiful woman on a date to a country music concert. That's all. One brief evening. And if you want to get back on the horse, so to speak, maybe a little uncomplicated sex?"

Joshua scowled. "I may be divorced and unemployed at the moment, but I sure as hell don't need my twin brother pimping me out to some strange woman. That's a *hell no* from me."

"You didn't let me finish. You'd be doing me a favor, honestly."

"How so?"

"Do you remember Layla Grandin?"

"Of course. How could I forget? She tagged along with us when we were kids. A cute tomboy. And as I recall, she grew up to be a very nice woman, though I haven't seen her in seven or eight years."

"Exactly. The trouble is, Dad has been meddling. He went to the reception after the funeral and chatted with Layla. You know how he's always wanted the two families to hook up."

"I do know that," Joshua said slowly. "But I married Becky and you—"

"I like variety," Jordan said quickly. "The thing is, Dad spun Layla some story about how he had concert tickets he can't use, and that I wanted to take Layla instead. But it was a lie."

"So the tickets are bogus?"

"The tickets are real. But I didn't know anything about it."

"So *you* take her. What's the big deal? It's only one night."

"I have plans," Jordan said. "And on top of that, don't you remember how Layla always had a crush on me?"

Joshua grimaced. "That's old history. Besides, I thought she was engaged."

"She was. A long time ago. You need to be better at keeping up with town gossip. Anyway, I don't know who ended it, but I hear Layla hasn't dated much or at all in the meantime. Maybe some guy broke her heart."

That thought bothered Joshua, but not enough to be sucked into one of his brother's wild schemes. "I just got back into town. I've got things to do."

"Come on, Josh. You're gonna need me in your corner. Ask Layla to the concert, pretend to be me, nicely of course. And then don't call her afterward. I'll be in the clear with Dad. Layla will get the message that I'm not into her. And you'll be free to get back on your feet here in Royal. It will be fun, I swear."

"It's too complicated. What kind of arrangements have you made with her?"

Jordan's expression was triumphant. "That's the best part. None, yet. The concert is Sunday night. All you have to do is text her that you'll pick her up at six. Feed her dinner. Take her to the venue. Drop her off later. Unless the sex thing is a possibility."

"I'm not going to make Layla Grandin a one-night stand." Joshua bristled.

"Aw, hell, baby brother. You know I was kidding about the sex. Will you do it? Dad will kill me if I mess up his grand plan. He's already put the ticket stuff in my name. But I have a very special lady on the hook for tomorrow night, and I don't want to disappointment her."

Joshua felt the urge to say yes. He and Jordan used to pull this trick on Layla all the time, but she always saw through them. It might be fun to try one more twin swap for old times' sake.

"Fine," he said. "I'll do it. But what makes you think she won't catch on that it's me and not you?"

"Layla and I haven't run in the same circles in a long time. I was at the funeral today, but not the reception, so she didn't see me. Your hair is a tad shorter than mine, and you're not as tanned as me, but other than that, we could still fool ninety-five percent of the people on any given day."

"Layla was always smarter than either you *or* me," Joshua said. "I might crash and burn, but it will be fun trying."

* * *

Layla glanced at the text on her phone for what must have been the twentieth time.

Looking forward to the concert. I'll pick you up at six. Dinner first. J.B.

Jordan Banks. Her childhood crush. Clearly, the senior Mr. Banks had orchestrated all of this. Jordan had had plenty of opportunities to ask Layla out over the years if he had been interested, but he hadn't. He wouldn't have suddenly invited her to a concert out of the blue if his father hadn't pressured him.

But even knowing that, Layla didn't mind. She needed a distraction.

Deciding what to wear had taxed the limits of her wardrobe. She wasn't really into the country music scene, but everyone in the world knew who Parker Brett was. Tonight's crowd would be upscale, wealthy and dressed to the nines.

Ticket prices were astronomical. Some radio personalities criticized Brett for ignoring his blue-collar base, but Layla didn't know if that was true or not. Parker gave incredibly generous donations to a host of charitable organizations, so who was she to judge?

Not much in her closet seemed appropriate for a concert. It was May. In Texas. Concert venues were notoriously hot and crowded. After some digging, she found an item she had bought and never worn. The halter-necked, button-up lightweight denim dress ended several inches above her knees and had a deep V-neck. She added red espadrilles that laced up over her ankles and a tiny leather purse that swung from a very long strap.

When she glanced in the mirror, she looked like a woman intent on having fun.

The dress bared a lot of skin. But with her wavy blond hair down tonight, she wouldn't feel too self-conscious. She added enough shadow and mascara to emphasize her blue eyes, then topped off her makeup with a light cherry stain and lip gloss.

Jewelry wasn't hard. She loved the large diamond hoop earrings her parents had given her for college graduation. They provided the final touch of glam to her appearance. She even added a dainty gold chain with a tiny diamond star.

Once she was ready and headed downstairs, it was hard not to freak out. For one thing, this was a date. With a man. After a long dry spell. For another, it was Jordan. Her crush on him had always been a combo of childhood nostalgia and female appreciation for a guy who was tall and handsome and charismatic.

As kids, she and the Banks boys had often been mistaken for siblings by strangers. Jordan's dirty-blond hair and blue eyes were enough like hers to make that a possibility. In some ways, she *had* felt like the twins were brothers.

They tolerated her and hung out with her and taught her how to climb trees and throw a baseball. Her own brother, Vic, had been a year younger than she was. Layla had always preferred the company of Jordan and Joshua, maybe because they made her feel grown-up and like she *belonged*.

At home, Vic was the only boy. Chelsea was the oldest, and Morgan the baby. Layla had always felt a bit like the odd man out. Honestly, she still felt that way even now.

When the doorbell rang, she sucked in a sharp breath and opened it. Jordan Banks stood on the veranda looking sexy enough to give any woman heart palpitations. Dark dress jeans molded to his long, muscular legs. His white, button-down shirt with sleeves rolled to the elbow emphasized his golden skin, and his hair was just tousled enough to make him look as if he had recently climbed out of bed.

She was mortified to feel her cheeks flushing. "Hi, Jordan," she said brightly. Maybe too brightly, because she saw him react. A tiny flinch? She couldn't exactly pin it down.

At last, he returned the smile. "Hey, Layla. It's good to see you. And man, you look gorgeous."

His sincere compliment soothed a few of the butterflies in her stomach. "Thank you." She closed the door behind her. "I'm looking forward to the concert."

"Me, too," he said. This time, the words weren't entirely convincing.

As he helped her into the car, she grimaced. "Listen, Jordan. I know your dad put you up to this. We don't have to go if you don't want to."

He slid behind the wheel and gave her an unreadable glance. "Don't be silly. You're a good friend. We've known each other forever." He paused. "I'm really sorry about your grandfather. I remember how much you loved him."

Layla's jaw wobbled, taking her by surprise. "Thanks," she said huskily. "It's hit me harder than I expected. I guess I thought he was immortal."

Jordan leaned forward and caught a tear that had escaped and clung to her lower lashes. "He must have been so proud of you."

For a split second, the air inside the car was charged with *something*. Layla shivered inwardly. She had always crushed on Jordan, but this was different. His tenderness reached the grief deep inside her chest and made her feel a little less devastated.

She swallowed hard. "I'm not going to fall apart on you," she said. "I swear."

His smile was lopsided. His left arm rested across the top of the steering wheel. "It would be okay if you did."

In that moment, she *knew* why this felt so weird and different. In a good way.

This wasn't *Jordan*.

The man gazing at her with such empathy was *Joshua*.

She would almost bet her life on it. But why? What was the point of this kind of subterfuge?

Years ago, the twins had often fooled teachers and classmates. They had tried their twin switch on Layla, too—all the time. Pranks. Silly fun. Nothing like this. Why would one brother pretend to be the other on a date?

Could she possibly be wrong?

Yet the more she stared at the man in the driver's seat, the less he looked like Jordan. Physically, yes, of course. They were two sides of the same penny.

But where Jordan was an extrovert and the life of any party, Joshua was the quieter, more thoughtful brother. The strong silent type.

Because she wasn't a hundred percent sure, she felt vulnerable. If this was a joke, it wasn't funny. Not at all.

"Shouldn't we be going?" she asked stiffly.

Jordan seemed to emerge from some kind of haze. He even shook his head slightly. "Of course. I made a reservation at Sheen."

"Oh, good. I love it there." Sheen was the perfect choice for a nondate date. The ambience was upscale and comfortable, but the tables didn't have the kind of shadowy intimacy that would have made the evening awkward.

By the time they were seated, Layla had relaxed some. If she was wrong, and the man across the table from her was Jordan, she would simply enjoy the evening. If he was Joshua, surely he would come clean eventually. In the meantime, she was determined to chill and have fun.

While they waited for their server to bring salads, Layla folded her hands in her lap. "Your father told me you were at the funeral. Thanks for coming. I'm afraid I didn't see you. It was packed."

"I was happy to be there," he said. "I'm sorry a prior commitment kept me from attending the reception afterward."

"Don't worry about it. Though you did miss some very good food."

He grinned. "Your mother always did cater a great meal."

"How are things at *your* ranch?" she asked.

Once again, she saw a tiny flinch. A weird look in his eyes. "Same as usual, I guess. Dad is always trying new stuff."

"I remember that about him."

"I suppose Victor Junior will be free to try new things, too."

Layla wrinkled her nose. "Oh, yes. He was always so frustrated by what he called my grandfather's *old-fashioned ways*. No telling what he'll be up to in the next few months. New feed, new bulls. The sky's the limit."

By the time they started on their second course, Layla was delighted with her decision to get out of the house. She was almost certain the man across the table from her was Joshua. He was thoughtful and funny. Their discussion of politics and books and movies was wide-ranging. But the most surprising aspect of the evening was how she responded to her escort physically. His overt masculinity made her shiver. She felt sexually aware of him in a way she hadn't done with any man in a long, long time.

Jordan's company might have been equally enjoyable but in a different way. Jordan would have been telling jokes and bantering with the waitress. Jordan would have flirted more. Maybe that was the origin of Layla's preadolescent crush. It had felt good to have a boy recognize the fact that she was a female.

At the concert venue, Jordan (or Joshua) kept his arm around her waist, holding her close in the midst of the crush. They each had very official-looking credentials that gave them VIP access and seating. Her date's name badge clearly said Jordan Banks. But Layla wasn't convinced.

Backstage, Layla did her best not to act like a gushing fan, even when she was introduced to the A-list movie star who was currently dating Parker Brett. When the woman's handler offered to take a photo of Jordan and Layla with Parker's lady friend, Layla almost betrayed her total fangirl status.

But she held on to her composure with an act of will. She wouldn't embarrass her date by being incredibly gushy and unsophisticated. After the photo op, Jordan and Layla were invited to partake of the buffet spread out on tables.

Because they had already eaten dinner, they skipped the main course offerings and instead sampled the desserts.

Jordan/Joshua grinned when she indulged in

cream puffs. "You have whipped topping on your chin," he said.

Before she could react, he picked up his napkin and leaned in to remove the sticky, sweet mess.

They were so close for a moment she could stare into the depths of his Texas bluebonnet eyes. The shade was lighter at the edges of his irises and deeper as it moved toward his pupils. Very distinctive.

They were sitting on folding chairs in a corner. It was still noisy, but for the moment, a bubble of privacy surrounded them.

As much fun as she was having, Layla couldn't forget about the fact that her "date" might not be who he was supposed to be. The uncertainty threatened to dampen the evening. She felt some definite chemistry with the man at her side, but her crush used to be on Jordan. Was she now flirting with *Joshua*? Because she so badly wanted to know, she decided to grill Jordan/Joshua. Maybe he would crack.

"So tell me about your brother," she said lightly. "What is Joshua up to? Still living in Dallas?"

This time she wasn't imagining the subtle reaction. The tiniest flinch. A stricken look in his gaze.

"Well, um," he said. "He's doing okay. In fact, he just came back to Royal very recently."

"Oh, how nice. Was Joshua at the funeral, too?"

Now Jordan/Joshua's face and neck turned red. He gulped his wine. "He wanted to be. But he had an important appointment at the bank. I think he may buy a house."

"So this is permanent? What about his wife? Am I remembering that right? Didn't he get married? It's been so long since I've seen him."

Layla should have felt guilty. The poor guy looked hunted. But if the Banks men thought they could pull this old trick on her, they deserved what they got. Let the games begin!

Her date paled now. "Joshua is divorced," he said.

"Oh, I'm so sorry."

He shrugged. "Becky was interested in the Banks money. Once Josh took a job in Dallas and decided not to accept any financial support from the ranch, she showed her true colors. He tried. Nobody likes to fail at marriage. But Becky wasn't interested."

Layla found herself confused. If this really was Joshua, he was being remarkably open with her. The words about his marriage were raw. She could understand his pain. Although she hadn't made it to the altar, she had thought her engagement was the beginning of a bright future.

She glanced at her watch. It was almost time to take their seats for the concert.

Jordan/Joshua leaned forward with an expression of urgency. "How about you, Layla? Any men in your life at the moment? Present company excluded." His lopsided smile made her pulse beat faster.

"I was engaged," she said slowly.

"Was?"

"My fiancé had a wandering eye."

"Ouch."

"Unfortunately, his other body parts followed."

Her companion winced. "I'm sorry."

"Thanks, but honestly, I was lucky. Being lied to is no fun. At least I found out before it was too late."

Jordan/Joshua looked desperate now. "I need to tell you something, Layla…"

Suddenly, the lights dimmed, and a bell dinged. Backstage visitors began moving toward the concert hall. Again, Jordan kept her close, his big strong body shielding her from getting stepped on.

Their seats were the best in the house—a box above and adjacent to the stage. From this vantage point, Layla could see everything, even Parker Brett's white teeth and sexy smile when he strode out onto the stage.

There was no opening musical act. Parker took command of the venue and the evening and didn't let loose for a full two and a half hours. He played all his familiar favorites plus a half-dozen new numbers.

Layla loved it. There was something about the energy of a live performance that couldn't be replicated. It was sorcery. During a slow, romantic ballad near the end of the evening, Jordan/Joshua slid an arm behind her shoulders, resting it on the back of her seat. Not touching. Just close.

It didn't mean anything. Just because Parker was singing about the spark between a man and a woman and the magic of new love… Coincidence. That was all.

She half turned in her seat, searching his face for the truth. "Thank you for bringing me," she said. "This is incredible."

Three

Joshua was in hell. He'd spent the entire concert watching Layla's expressive face. Parker Brett was a damned fine entertainer, but Josh couldn't take his eyes off the woman at his side. When Layla laughed, Josh got a funny feeling in the pit of his stomach. It felt a lot like desperation and desire.

His divorce had sent his libido into hiding for a very long time. Now he felt himself stretching, waking up from a long, painful sleep.

As they walked to the car, Layla talked nonstop. He caught whiffs of her light perfume occasionally, but it was watching her hair dance in the breeze that really got to him. The dress she wore was not particularly outrageous. Still, the way it hugged her modest curves and bared her long, toned legs made his mouth dry.

She was wearing red sandal-y things that gave her three or four extra inches in height. He couldn't help thinking that he and Layla would be a perfect match in bed. Or standing. Or pressing their bodies together in any one of a dozen other positions he could imagine.

He was sweating by the time they made it to the car, but it had nothing to do with the muggy spring night. After he unlocked her door, he rounded the car and opened the driver's side.

Suddenly, the intimacy ratcheted up about a thousand percent. "I'll turn on the AC," he said. He had to tell her the truth. It was the right thing, the only thing to do. But he didn't want the night to end with her being pissed at him.

According to Jordan's dumb plan, Joshua was supposed to wrap up the evening by saying *I'll call you*. Then Jordan *wouldn't* call. Layla would think her date was a jerk. End of story.

Maybe that was the way to go. Let this fiction play itself out. Then in a few days, Joshua could make arrangements to bump into Layla as himself. The two of them could start with a clean slate.

The trouble was, he was terrible at this kind of subterfuge. He'd been known to ruin surprise parties without meaning to…he sucked at poker. Anything that required evasion or deception was not his strong suit.

He started the car. Soon, cool air blew on their faces. It didn't help Joshua at all.

Hang on, he told himself. *Work the plan.* Jordan's plan, damn it. Why had he ever let his brother talk him into this frustrating night? It was supposed to be lighthearted fun, not sexual torture.

As they made their way through the darkened streets of downtown Royal, Layla carried the conversation, for sure. He hoped he made sense when he responded. Actually, he didn't remember saying anything at all, but he must have.

When they finally made it beyond the town limits and out to the sprawling Grandin ranch, he pulled up in front of the beautiful main house, shut off the engine and took a deep breath. "We're here," he said.

Wow. Not smooth at all.

The ranch was quiet. There were lights on in the very back of the house and upstairs, but here in the driveway, the only illumination came from the moonlight filtering through the windshield.

Layla half turned in her seat. "Thanks for taking me to the concert, *Jordan*. I had a lot of fun."

His brain raced. Had Layla deliberately emphasized his brother's name? Did she know the truth? If so, Joshua needed to come clean now. She had been lied to before…by someone important in her life. Joshua didn't want to add to her pain or reinforce her opinion of loser guys who couldn't tell the truth, even if tonight's ruse was meant to be a nod to their childhood game of twin switch.

I'll call you. That was what he was supposed to say. Three little words.

He couldn't make his lips form the syllables. If he had never left Royal and moved to Dallas, maybe he would have eventually asked Layla to go out with him. It could have happened.

He reined in his imagination and focused on the present. He hadn't had sex in twenty months, two weeks and three days. His life was in ruins. Layla represented everything he wanted in a just-for-fun relationship.

But it wouldn't be fair to play around with her. Not at all.

Three words. That's all he had to say. *I'll call you.*

She was looking at him oddly. Had she asked *him* a question? Was she waiting for an answer?

He shifted in his seat, wanting to jump out of the car and howl at the moon. Why had he let Jordan talk him into this? The mischievous twin switch had turned into an evening of sexual hunger.

Layla's smile faded. Moments before, she had been animated and friendly. Now her expression was definitely wary. "Are you okay, Jordan?" she asked.

Her head cocked to one side. She eyed him like a science experiment she needed to study. To analyze.

When she called him Jordan he ground his teeth. He wasn't Jordan. Never had been. This was a heck of a time to remind himself that young Layla Grandin had once had a crush on *Jordan* Banks, not Joshua.

Truthfully, it was Jordan, not Joshua, who had always juggled two or three beautiful girls or women at one time. They flocked to him. He made them laugh. Made them feel special. Joshua wasn't jealous of his brother's charisma. His own hard-to-get personality had snagged him plenty of women. But right now, he wouldn't mind having a smidgen of his sibling's easy charm.

"Jordan?"

If Layla Grandin said that name one more time, he was liable to snap. His blood boiled in his veins. He was frustrated with the dumb twin switch and desperately attracted to the woman he had taken on a faux date this evening.

"Layla?" He said her name gruffly, wishing he could blurt out the truth. But his original plan was best. Let this "Jordan" relationship expire, and then Joshua could swoop in and play cleanup batter.

"Yes?" Her smile was tentative now. Perhaps the tone of his voice had spooked her. It was hard for a guy to play it cool when every cell in his body wanted the woman sitting two feet away.

"Will you have dinner with me tomorrow night?"

What the hell? Where did that come from? No way was he going to let "Jordan" go out with Layla again.

He sensed her ambivalence. His weird behavior was freaking out even him. "Say yes," he urged. Her silence wasn't a good sign.

Finally, she twisted a strand of hair between her fingers and sighed. "I honestly didn't think you enjoyed yourself this evening," she said quietly. "I know tonight's arrangement wasn't your idea. Why would you want to do it again?"

The vulnerability in her words squeezed his heart. "I had a great time," he said. "I don't know what you're talking about."

"Jordan, I—"

Hearing his brother's name on Layla's lips made him snap. Jordan had plenty of women. This one was off-limits. Besides, Jordan himself had passed her off on Joshua. What kind of way was that to treat a sweet, sexy woman like Layla?

"Please," he muttered. "We need to talk."

A tiny frown appeared between her brows. "You said that earlier. Right before the concert started."

Now he had boxed himself into a corner. How could he let "Jordan" ride off into the sunset if Joshua made a big deal about *talking*? Was he going to tell Layla the truth tomorrow night?

She touched his hand. Briefly. Placating him. "I'd like to, but I can't. Our family has a very important meeting at the lawyer's office Monday at seven. It was the only time we were all free to get together. There's a bit of trouble about the estate."

Joshua frowned. "Tuesday night, then?" Without overthinking it, he leaned in, slid his hand beneath her hair and kissed her soft, shiny pink lips.

He'd watched her reapply the gloss after dinner and again after the backstage buffet. It was a simple feminine action. Nothing overtly erotic. But it had made him hard.

Now he discovered the gloss tasted like peppermint.

The kiss deepened for a nanosecond before he pulled back. He didn't want to kiss her as Jordan, but he hadn't been able to wait another minute.

"Should I apologize for that?" he asked gruffly.

Layla touched her lips with the fingers of one hand. He wasn't sure she realized she had done it. "No apologies," she said. Her gaze was wide-eyed. Had he shocked her? Wouldn't *Jordan* have kissed a beautiful woman on a first date?

"So dinner?" He repeated the invitation.

Her silence lasted long enough to make him squirm. "Sure. Text me tomorrow night and I'll see if I'm free Tuesday. It should be fine."

Joshua's personal life had been in the pits for so long, it was shocking to realize he was actually looking forward to something. "Don't change your mind," he said.

She grinned. "I've known you a long time, Jordan. Do you ever remember me being flighty?"

This time he was almost sure she emphasized the word *Jordan*. Did she know which brother she was talking to? And if so, why hadn't she said anything?

Maybe for the same reasons he hadn't. Maybe they were both wary. A failed marriage. A broken engagement. Neither of them was batting a thousand in the relationship department. And they weren't getting any younger.

Layla gathered her purse and stepped out of the car. He hopped out, too, and eyed her over the top of the vehicle. In the moonlight, she looked younger.

"Good night, Layla," he said.

She blew him a kiss. "Good night."

He could have left. But he lingered to watch her ascend the broad set of stairs that led to the porch. When she opened the front door and disappeared inside, he sighed. This had been the best night he'd had in forever.

But he had screwed it up.

He was determined to set things straight as soon as possible. If he could exit this twin switch gracefully, maybe he had a shot at coaxing Layla into his bed. Even as a kid, he had always wanted to one-up his brother, just for bragging rights. Now the stakes were higher and far more personal.

Layla found Chelsea watching a movie in the den. "Where is everybody?" she asked, sinking into her favorite chair and taking off her shoes.

"You look super cute," Chelsea said. "Mom and Dad went upstairs an hour ago. Grandma, too. Vic and Morgan are out on a double date with some friends of theirs. How was the concert?"

"Actually, it was great." Layla could feel her cheeks burn, especially since her older sister eyed her with a grin.

"So being set up by two old men wasn't a bust?"

"Jordan was nice about it. Parker Brett's concert was amazing. I had a good time."

"Why do I hear a *but* in there somewhere?"

"You'll think I'm crazy."

"No more than usual." Chelsea laughed at her own joke. "What aren't you telling me? Did you do the nasty with Jordan Banks?"

"On the first date? Of course not."

"Lots of women do."

"Not me."

"Then what has you all riled up?"

Layla fiddled with the hem of her dress. "I'm almost positive the man I went out with tonight was *Joshua* Banks, not Jordan."

Chelsea sat up straighter and turned off the TV. "You can't be serious."

"I am. I realized it in the first hour we were together. I know those twins. They may look identical, but their personalities are completely different."

"Did you say something?"

"No. Because I wasn't a hundred percent sure. I haven't seen either of them in a very long time."

"But I thought Joshua lived in Dallas. And was married."

"He did. But he's back. Divorced, unfortunately."

Chelsea wrinkled her nose. "Sucks for him, but it sounds like you should be glad he's single again. I haven't seen you this flustered in ages."

"I'm not flustered," Layla lied.

"Riiiggghht…"

It was impossible to fool a sister who had known you forever.

Layla decided to change the subject. "How's everybody doing after the big bombshell?"

"Daddy's freaking out, of course. And he's mad as hell. Mom spends all her time trying to calm him down. Vic and Morgan don't seem to care. Uncle Daniel was supposed to fly back to Paris, but Daddy forbade him to leave until we sort this out."

"*Forbade?* Good grief, we're not the royal family."

Chelsea snorted. "Our male parental unit has let his new position as patriarch go to his head already."

"So Uncle Daniel stayed?"

"Only until Tuesday morning."

"I don't really want to go sit in a lawyer's office," Layla confessed. "They give me the heebie-jeebies."

"I don't want to go either, but it's a command performance."

Layla rubbed her temple where a headache was beginning to brew. "Do you think our family is weird?"

Chelsea rolled her eyes. "Can I plead the Fifth?"

"I'm serious. Is it strange that we all live under one roof?"

"This place is sixteen thousand square feet. With another five thousand in the guest house. We each practically have our own suites anyway."

"I guess. But what about Vic? He always has a woman in his life. Shouldn't he want more privacy?"

"Ewww." Chelsea shuddered. "I do *not* want to talk about our brother's sex life."

"But why does he stay here? Shouldn't an unattached male want his own place?"

Chelsea shook her head slowly. "Sometimes I forget how sweet and naive you are. Believe me, Layla. I'm pretty sure our dear brother has had an apartment in town somewhere for a long time."

"But why does he still make the pretense of living here?"

"You know he likes being the favored son and grandson. He wants control of the ranch to come to him someday. Squatter's rights dictate that he shouldn't stray too far from Daddy's sphere."

"I suppose."

"We all have plenty of our own money. Any of us could leave if we wanted to. Is that it, Lay-Lay? Are you feeling the need to spread your wings?"

For some reason, hearing the childhood nickname made Layla teary-eyed. "No," she said. "I don't want to leave. At least not right now. I'm like Vic, I guess. I keep hoping Daddy will eventually see that you and I have as much right to run the ranch as his precious son."

"I wouldn't bet on it. Apparently, having a penis is a prerequisite for being a real rancher in Texas."

The sarcasm made Layla smile. "Or at least here in Royal." Layla yawned. "I'm beat. I'm gonna take a shower and go to bed."

"My movie is almost over. I'll be up in a bit."

As Layla climbed the stairs, she pondered Chelsea's half-serious question. *Did* she want to get her own place? Sometimes it might be nice to avoid all the drama.

In the bathroom, she undressed and had to avoid looking at herself in the mirror. She kept remembering the feel of a warm male hand cupping the side of her neck ever so briefly. Try as she might, she couldn't convince herself that the man at her side tonight was Jordan Banks.

If he was *Joshua*, what did that mean? Why the switch? Bertram Banks had mentioned Layla's adolescent crush. So clearly, the older man had no clue his boys had something up their sleeves.

As she climbed into bed and turned out the light, she moved restlessly under the sheet. When she closed her eyes, all she could see were those beautiful blue irises, the spark of humor and desire. Was it really desire?

She'd been fooled once.

She couldn't afford to be so stupid a second time.

But even after giving herself a stern lecture, she had a feeling she was going to dream about the man who had kissed her tonight...

Four

Lawyer's offices were about as bad as funeral homes. Layla drove her own car to the meeting. She'd had drinks and dinner with a girlfriend earlier, so she had promised to meet the family here. When she walked in, the mood was glacial and uncomfortable.

Layla took a seat beside Chelsea and prepared for a long, boring hour. Hopefully not more than that. As she scanned the room, she saw that most everyone had showed up, including her grandmother. Uncle Trent and Aunt Lisa were noticeably absent. Maybe because they didn't have anything to gain or lose, they had chosen not to attend.

The lawyer was in his late sixties or early seventies. His silver hair and conventional clothing made him the epitome of upscale legal representation. He had worked for the Grandin family for decades.

"I'll get right to the point," he said. "I've contacted the attorney who prepared those papers you received on the day of the funeral. He has apologized for sending them at such a stressful moment for your entire family. Claims he didn't know."

Layla's father bristled. "And you believe him?"

"I have no reason not to." The lawyer addressed Layla's grandmother. "Mrs. Grandin. Did your husband ever mention anything about oil rights?"

Miriam straightened in her chair. She was a tough woman, and one who had remained in the shadow of her husband's forceful personality. "Never that I recall. But Victor kept his own counsel. If he took anyone into his confidence, it would have been Augustus Lattimore. Those two old men were thick as thieves."

Again, Layla's father was visibly upset. Layla felt sorry for him actually. It must have been hard to be shut out of all the decision-making. He was at an age where some men began to think about retiring in a few years. But Victor Junior was just now getting his chance to be in charge of the ranch.

Would *he* cling to control for three more decades? Like his father had?

Vic spoke up. "We don't really have anything to worry about, do we? Isn't this probably a scam? Anyone with a good digital printer can produce documents."

Chelsea nodded. "And according to the internet, if you wad up your paper and soak it in tea, you can make it look old."

Bethany Grandin glanced at her daughter. "Good grief, Chelsea. You're letting your imagination run away with you."

The lawyer must have sensed he was losing control of this session. He cleared his throat. "Let's stick to what we know. I asked Thurston's legal counsel for additional information about this situation." He directed his attention to Layla's uncle. "Mr. Grandin. Thurston claims you had an affair with his mother, Cynthia." The accusation was blunt.

Daniel shrugged, looking almost defiant. "Years ago. So what?"

The lawyer grimaced as if he had been hoping for a denial. "There was a baby. A girl. Ashley."

Daniel shook his head. "I did have a brief relationship with Cynthia—when I was in Royal for a couple of months. But there was no pregnancy." He ran a hand across the back of his neck, betraying his unease. He was solidly built though thinner than Layla remembered. His hair was going gray, but his dark brown eyes were the same. Layla wasn't close to her uncle, because he had lived in France for decades.

The lawyer continued. "So, you have no knowledge of this alleged child?"

Layla's uncle didn't look happy. "I do not," he said curtly. "I won't deny having a physical relationship with Cynthia Thurston many years ago. But I had no further contact with her after that."

"Is it possible she couldn't find you to tell you there was a baby on the way?"

Victor scowled. "My brother has lived in France for a long time. But he has never been off the grid. Any of us could have been in touch with him if this woman asked us to intervene. The timing of the whole claim is suspect."

Layla wondered privately if her uncle's lover would have been too embarrassed to contact a family as well-known and influential as the Grandins. Maybe she decided to handle things on her own.

Layla spoke up. "Daddy, I think you're forgetting something. Cynthia and Ashley were killed in a car crash a couple of years ago. Heath and Nolan may have just now stumbled onto these papers."

The lawyer nodded. "Anything is possible. However, Thurston is intimating that the oil rights were due Ashley, because she was a Grandin by birth. I'm still looking into why the Lattimore ranch was included. I have a call in to their lawyer. The burden of proof is on the other side. That buys you some time. I know you're thinking of hiring an investigator. Probably a good idea. We can all keep digging. Ms. Miriam, perhaps you could look through your husband's papers for any clues."

"I'd be happy to…"

After that, the meeting adjourned, and the room began to empty.

Layla realized her uncle was standing alone. She approached him and put a hand on his shoulder. "I'm so sorry," she said. "You must be in shock."

He nodded slowly. She could see the stunned bafflement in his gaze. "It's bad enough to find out I fathered a child and Cynthia didn't say a word. But it's killing me that it's too late. I can't do a damn thing about it. I can't ask Cynthia for an explanation, and I can't get to know Ashley. I would have been better off not knowing."

Moments later, Layla left him, sensing that he preferred to defer his emotions until he had privacy to think about the situation.

She said a word to Chelsea and then headed out to where her car was parked on the street. All evening she had wanted to glance at her texts, but she made herself resist. Now was the time. She slid into the driver's seat, shut the door and turned on the engine so the car would cool down.

Then she checked her phone. She sucked in a breath. There it was…

As promised. I'm checking in about dinner tomorrow night. J.B.

Layla couldn't help but smile. Even if this rendezvous resulted in an awkward moment of truth, she didn't want to miss it. First of all, she wanted to satisfy her curiosity about which of the Banks boys had taken her to the concert. And second—because she was almost positive it was Joshua—she wanted to see if the spark of attraction was more than a fluke.

She responded quickly...

I'm free! What time?

Are you up for a picnic? If so, I'll pick you up at 5, and we'll go for a drive...can you supply a quilt?

Layla was surprised, but she had no objections. A picnic would give them more privacy to clear the air.

Sounds good to me. See you then...

She tossed her phone in her purse so she wouldn't be tempted to continue the conversation. She probably should be mad. Mad at either or both of the Banks men. But maybe it was a harmless prank. She hoped so. She would give them the benefit of the doubt, mostly because she wanted to explore the tantalizing sparks she had experienced last night.

The following day, she was busy with a million and one things around the ranch. And she spared a couple of hours to help her grandmother. Miriam was intent on donating her husband's clothing as soon as possible. It was her way of coping with grief.

The two women sorted through hangers and checked pockets. The only things they found were old pieces of hard butterscotch candy, still in the wrappers.

Layla put her arms around her grandmother at one point and hugged her. "I'm so sorry about Grandy. Are you going to be okay?"

Miriam nodded, wiping her eyes. "Oh, yes. But he and I were together so long, it feels like I've lost a limb. We had good days and bad, Layla. Still, the two of us were rock solid. I hardly know what to do with myself now."

"I promise we'll all be here for you, Grammy. I know this must be so very hard."

Later that afternoon, Layla showered and changed into a new sundress she had bought recently. The material was a pale yellow gauzy cotton scattered with tiny teal flowers. The spaghetti-strap bodice was lined, so she skipped a bra.

A picnic sounded sedate enough. She settled on cream leather ballet flats. They were more cute than practical. Not the thing for tramping around the ranch, but perfect for a date with a handsome man.

When Jordan/Joshua arrived at five on the nose, she went out to the porch and down the steps to meet him, not waiting for him to come up and ring the doorbell. There were too many unanswered questions. The last thing she wanted was for her nosy family to grill whichever of the Banks brothers was picking her up.

Her date shielded his eyes from the sun. "Hey, there."

"Hey, yourself." She handed him the quilt. Again, her gut feeling told her she was being greeted by

Joshua. Jordan was louder and more gregarious. This man gave her a tight smile, tucked her into the front seat of a luxury sports car and got in without saying another word. It was a different car tonight. Had the other one been Jordan's?

To be honest, Layla didn't mind that the drive was mostly silent. It had been a long, stressful week. She was happy to lean back and take a deep breath.

The car was a dream. Top-of-the-line engineering and every possible creature comfort. It was also a stick shift. Outside town when they found a two-lane road that was straight and deserted, the man behind the wheel hit the gas.

Layla smiled. There was something about speed that helped wash away tension and stress. It was one reason she liked riding horses. But today was even more exciting. She could feel the powerful engine as it worked its way higher and higher.

Watching her companion out of the corner of her eye was entertaining in its own way. Though he might not even know it, the tiny smile that tipped up the corners of his masculine lips told Layla he was enjoying himself.

He was dressed beautifully, but casually. Well-worn jeans showcased long legs, a narrow waist and powerful thighs. His expensive tooled-leather cowboy boots were the real deal. The navy-and-yellow-plaid cotton shirt was soft, the sleeves rolled to his elbows.

He also smelled really, really good.

Layla didn't ask where they were headed. It was nice to sit back and let someone else steer the ship for a change. She was, unfortunately, a bit of a workaholic. It was a tendency made even worse in the wake of her broken engagement. She had buried herself in work and scarcely come up for air.

Now she felt her muscles going lax, her body nestling into the embrace of a butter-soft leather seat. Even her bones seemed willing to loosen and unkink. Drowsy contentment wrapped her in a cocoon of well-being.

Joshua didn't know whether to be insulted or amused when he realized his passenger was asleep. She had kicked off one shoe and tucked her leg beneath her. In that position, her dress rode up, revealing a tanned, toned thigh.

His hands tightened on the wheel. He had no idea how this picnic was going to play out, but he hoped Layla would give him a chance to explain. He wasn't looking forward to confessing the twin switch, but it had to be done.

When he stopped the car at last, they were parked atop a low rise miles from the nearest house. This property was for sale. He had toyed with the idea of buying it. But such a decision would mean staying in Royal, and he wasn't sure he was ready to commit to that.

He studied Layla as she slept, glad of the opportunity to catalog how the young tomboy had morphed into a capable, extremely feminine woman. Her hair was still the golden blond he remembered. From his close vantage point, it looked soft and silky.

His sex stirred, reminding him that a man his age shouldn't be sleeping alone. Layla was the first woman in forever to tempt him. Seriously tempt him.

The dress she wore wasn't meant to be provocative. But it bared her arms and shoulders. Her legs were bare, too. In fact, she was probably completely bare underneath except for whatever underwear she wore.

Since he could see the tiny outline of her nipples, maybe nothing but panties.

He gripped the steering wheel and told himself he had to keep a rein on his baser impulses. For one thing, Layla thought she was out on a date with Jordan. And for another, if he wanted Layla's forgiveness, he couldn't seduce her on this gorgeous spring afternoon, no matter how much he wanted to...

He said her name quietly, not wanting to startle her. "Layla. Wake up, Layla. We're here."

It took three tries, and on the last one he actually shook her shoulder. The feel of her delicate bones and soft skin seared itself into his fingertips.

Layla yawned and opened her eyes. He witnessed the exact moment she realized what had happened. Her whole face turned red.

"Oh, gosh," she whispered, scrubbing her hands over her cheeks and straightening her hair. "I'm so sorry. Did I fall asleep on you?"

"Not *on* me," he teased. "But beside me, yes."

When he realized she was genuinely mortified, he chuckled. "Don't sweat it, Layla. You've had several hard days. I'm glad you felt comfortable enough with me to relax. You must have needed the rest."

"I haven't been sleeping at night," she admitted. The embarrassed color faded, leaving her pale.

"How is your grandmother doing?" he asked.

"I helped her pack up Grandy's clothes today. She's hanging in there."

Joshua rubbed his chin. "Isn't that kind of quick?"

Layla's smile was wistful. "You'd have to know my grandmother. She's sort of the rip-off-the-bandage type."

"Everyone deals with grief differently, I suppose." He thought about his marriage—the separations, the long arguments…the realization that he couldn't save the relationship with Becky on his own. He had grieved.

Layla sat up and reached for her shoe, then slid her foot into it and adjusted the heel. "I seem to remember you promising me a picnic?"

He nodded. Layla was hurting, too, but she was very independent. "I did, indeed. The basket is in the trunk."

Both of them exited the car. Layla stretched and looked around.

They were parked amidst a small copse of cottonwood trees. Years ago, there might have been a small creek at the base of the rise, but it had long since dried up.

"This is nice," she said, giving him a smile that made him catch his breath.

He wanted Layla Grandin on several levels, but there was a hurdle he had to clear first. He wasn't sure what he was going to say, but sooner was better than later.

While he marshalled his thoughts, he spread out the beautiful thick quilt that had probably been handed down through the Grandin family. Though it was faded, the patina of age added charm. Unlike Layla, he and Jordan had no living grandparents. Nor a mother. Only their pushy, upwardly mobile father who had always aspired to be more than what he was.

Nothing wrong with that as long as a person understood acceptable boundaries. Bertram Banks was always pushing.

To be fair, Joshua couldn't blame his father for the current situation. Jordan could have said no to his father. Joshua could have said no to his brother. But he hadn't. Because a part of him had been intrigued.

When Layla sat down, her sundress settled around her like a patch of sunshine. She was graceful and unselfconscious. Joshua couldn't help thinking about the past. Some people might wonder why twin boys had allowed a younger playmate, a girl, to tag along on their adventures. As Joshua remembered it, the reasons were at least twofold.

Layla had kept up with them every step of the

way. And her presence—although she wasn't a girly girl back then—had been a way for the boys to show off, to continually try and best each other.

It was a pattern that had persisted over the years... though without their sidekick, of course.

Joshua opened the trunk and retrieved the large fancy picnic basket. "I ordered this from the Royal Diner. I hope I picked things you like. I did tell them no bananas in the fruit salad."

"I can't believe you remembered that I don't like bananas." Layla laughed, her eyes sparkling in the dappled shade. Though her irises were blue like his, the shade was different. Layla's were lighter with flecks of gold.

He toed off his boots and joined her on the blanket, crossing his sock-clad feet at the ankles. When he leaned back on his elbows, he sighed without meaning to. A weight he'd been carrying for months finally slipped away.

The past was the past. It was time for him to move on. He turned his head, looked at Layla. Took a deep breath. "I need to tell you something."

Her expression was both wistful and wry. "Is it that you're Joshua and not Jordan?"

Shock ran up and down his spine. He sat up, slinging an elbow over one knee. "You knew?"

She shrugged. "Not at first. But after half an hour, I was fairly certain. I haven't seen Jordan in a long time, nor you for that matter. So I had to question my gut feeling."

He frowned. "Not many people can tell us apart."

Layla gave him a look that questioned his intelligence. "I spent days and weeks and years running wild with you two when we were kids. I used to know you both very well."

"What gave me away?"

"Well, for starters, you're quieter than Jordan. Deeper maybe. He's a bit of a flirt."

Her comment stung, though Joshua was aware she hadn't meant it as a gibe. Becky had told him repeatedly that he was no fun. He'd heard it enough times that he eventually began to wonder if she was right.

"I'm sorry," he said, managing a grin. "Well, hell. If we're being honest, I'm not sorry at all. I had a great time with you at the concert."

"Me, too," she said. "But you still haven't explained why you and Jordan tried the twin switch with me."

"No big secret." He sighed. "Dad set all this in motion. But Jordan already had another date."

Her lips twitched. "Of course he did. I should have known."

"Otherwise, I'm sure he'd have been happy to take you to the concert."

"You don't know any such thing. I've seen the women your brother dates. I'm not exactly his type."

"Maybe." Joshua didn't want to wade into that one.

His confession hadn't extinguished the thread of heat between them. If anything, the *sizzle* intensified.

Layla tucked her hair behind her ear. "You want to start over?" she asked.

Joshua was struck by her response to the situation. She didn't sulk. She didn't hold a grudge. And she didn't punish him. Was this what normal, nice women were like? He had been ensnared with his ex-wife for so long, he had almost forgotten.

"I'd like that," he said.

"Let me help you set out the food."

They were both hungry. The conversation was lighthearted as they ate, but beneath the surface communication ran a vein of something else. Awareness.

He was in no place to jump back into anything serious. And he didn't know if Layla was the kind of woman to dabble in a short-term affair. But he was willing to find out.

She put him on the spot at one moment. "Was all that stuff you said to me the other night about your wife the truth? You know, when you were pretending to be your brother?"

He groaned. "You're not going to let me forget that, are you?"

Layla's grin was smug. "Probably not. At least for the moment."

"Yes," he said flatly. "It was true. My father warned me that Becky was after the family money. But I didn't listen."

"You were in love."

He shrugged. "I thought I was. I *wanted* to get married. I liked the idea of starting a family."

"But she never got pregnant?"

"Nope. In fact, she flatly refused to consider it. But that was the least of our problems. She loved Dallas, and the social life there. All she talked about was making the right connections, cultivating the right friends."

"And you?"

"I had a great job I loved—project manager for an energy company—but I had always assumed that one day we would go back to Royal and start a family. Unfortunately, I hadn't made those intentions clear *before* we got married. That was my mistake. I decided we should go to counseling and work on our problems. Becky agreed at first. We made it through three sessions, maybe four. But that was it. I discovered it's impossible for one person to save a marriage when the other partner doesn't care."

"I'm so sorry, Joshua." Her empathetic gaze made him feel marginally better. Rehashing his romantic past was not the way to impress a woman.

"It was for the best. We never really loved each other, I guess. We were separated for a little over two years. The divorce was final a few months ago."

Layla frowned. "But if you still loved your job, why are you here in Royal? Just for a visit?"

"Actually, I…"

"You what?" She prompted him when he couldn't get the words out.

"I quit my job. I told Jordan, but my father doesn't know."

"Wow. That's a big decision."

He gazed at her wryly. "After the divorce was final, I started feeling the pull of home, even more than I had before. I've missed the wide-open spaces. I think about the ranch a lot."

"What will your dad say?"

"Jordan thinks he'll take me back in a heartbeat."

"So, problem solved?"

"It's hard to tell. I don't want to step on Jordan's toes. I wonder if I should start over somewhere completely new."

Five

Layla was surprised by the sting of disappointment that settled in her stomach. She didn't even *know* the adult Joshua, not really. Yet maybe because of their childhood friendship, she felt a connection.

"If you don't mind a little amateur psychoanalysis on my part," she said, "I'll offer a theory."

He grimaced. "Feel free."

"I think you feel like a failure, and it has rattled your confidence."

Joshua blinked. His cheeks flushed. "You shoot straight, don't you?"

The rueful note in his words made her wonder if she had gone too far. "It's not a criticism," she said quickly. "But I've had some experience with the phenomenon. When I found out Richard was cheating on me, it shook me to the core. Here was a man I had chosen, a guy I was planning to spend my life with, and I had made a huge mistake."

"You and I are hardly the first or the last to misjudge other human beings."

"True. But up until then, I considered myself pretty smart and capable. Suddenly, everyone around me was giving me pitying glances. As if I was some poor, delicate creature. I hated it."

"I get that."

There was silence between them for a moment. Layla smoothed the skirt of her dress, not quite able to look at her companion. "I never thought this picnic was going to be a deep dive into our darkest emotions."

"Is that a bad thing? Maybe we've cleared the air."

"Maybe."

They finished their meal in companionable silence. Layla wondered if this was the last time she would see Joshua. She didn't often cross paths with the Banks family unless it was at some charity function or town event. If Joshua decided not to stay, this was it.

Something inside her wasn't willing to accept that. "You could do me a favor," she said. "If you're still around in a couple of weeks."

"What's that?"

"The Cattleman's Club is having their spring luncheon soon. I don't have a date, but I'd like to. You know how gossip in Royal is. I'm really tired of everyone discussing *poor little Layla*. They all know about Richard."

"I could do that," he said. "I'm still a member on paper. Though I haven't been inside that beautiful old building in years."

"You'll be surprised," she said. "We have an on-site day care now. And lots of other improvements. Change comes slowly, but it does eventually come."

"I take it your whole family belongs to the club?"

"We do."

"And how will things change at the ranch now that your grandfather is gone? You said your dad has been frustrated by your grandfather's old-fashioned ways."

"Ugh. Sore subject," she muttered.

"You don't have to discuss it if you don't want to."

"I don't mind. Dad is just as old-fashioned in his views, though he doesn't see it. It looks like I have a choice to make."

"Like how?"

"Chelsea and I are about to get sidelined, even though all either of us has ever wanted was to be an integral part of the ranch. She's furious about it. I'm more resigned to the inevitable, I guess. I train horses, and since my degree is in business, I keep an eye on the bottom line when no one is watching."

"Then what's the problem?"

"My father is fifty-nine years old, and he is just now getting a shot and running things his way. I don't know if my siblings and I are prepared to wait that long. It's frustrating when we have progressive new ideas, grounded in science, but Daddy won't listen. Grandy was the same in that regard, but at least he had the excuse of coming from a much older generation."

"Remind me how old your siblings are?"

"Chelsea is the eldest at thirty-five. I'm thirty-two, a year younger than you. Vic is thirty-one, and our baby sister, Morgan, is twenty-eight."

"Do all of them want to be significant parts of running the ranch?"

She grimaced. "Not Morgan. She owns a boutique in town. But it doesn't even matter. Vic has the edge in that sweepstakes."

"How so?"

"Grandy and my father were and are very patriarchal. Because Vic is the only boy, he's on deck to be the next lord of the manor."

"That doesn't seem fair at all." Joshua had reclined on his side. He looked sleepy and replete... but wickedly masculine. Layla realized she was both aroused by him and on her guard. Because Layla was lonely, and Josh was a huge part of her past, she might be tempted to wallow in sentimentality and sexual attraction and do something stupid.

"Enough about me," she said. "Maybe we should be getting back." The sun was sinking low in the sky, chasing the horizon.

"What's your hurry?" he asked with a teasing smile. That smile was deadly. It made all her secret vulnerable places tingle. As if a special kind of lightning was about to strike.

She cleared her throat. "No hurry. But I'm sure you have important things to do."

"Nothing more important than spending time with an interesting woman."

"Flatterer."

The smile disappeared. Now his gaze was warm, maybe even hot.

He played with the hem of her skirt, folding a tiny piece of fabric between his fingers. Layla was mesmerized, watching that big tanned hand so near her knee.

"Tell me something," he said, his voice deep and husky. "When I kissed you night before last, were you kissing Jordan?"

Yikes. Dangerous territory. She had a choice. Honesty or deflection. It was really no choice at all.

"No," she said. "I knew exactly who I was kissing. It was you, Josh."

The hot light in his eyes flared into male satisfaction. "Good." He leaned forward, curled a hand behind her neck and slanted his mouth over hers. No fumbling. Nothing tentative. Just a man intent on giving and receiving pleasure.

Somebody moaned. Probably her. Layla was too enmeshed in the magic of the moment to care. She trusted Joshua. She had always enjoyed his company. He was a decent, funny, kind man with a kick-ass body and worlds of experience.

Right now, he was everything she wanted.

Joshua deepened the kiss, his tongue stroking hers, his teeth nibbling her bottom lip. Eventually, he moved to her collarbone, pressing his lips to a particularly vulnerable spot. She caught her breath. Heat pooled in her sex. She wrapped her arms around his neck, trying to get closer.

She was ready to devour him, but her partner was being remarkably circumspect under the circumstances. Maybe he thought it was too soon.

"Do you have any condoms with you?" she asked.

When he froze, she felt humiliation engulf her in smothering waves. "Never mind," she muttered, pulling away abruptly. "That was the wine talking."

Joshua grasped her shoulders. His hands shook. His cheeks were flushed. "I do," he said. "But are you sure this is what you want?"

"Right now? Yes."

Her answer seemed to satisfy any doubts he had. Maybe this was reckless or even self-sabotaging, but Layla didn't care. She needed Joshua. She *wanted him*.

He eased her onto her back and leaned over her. One big masculine hand cupped her breast firmly. When her nipple peaked, he rubbed it, circling the taut point through the thin fabric of her dress.

Fire streaked through her, incinerating her doubts. She trembled, not because she was unsure, but because the magic of the moment left her breathless. If she was this strung out from a mere touch, how was she going to survive what happened next?

She had never considered herself a passive lover, but for the moment, she reveled in having Joshua take charge. He was sure of himself. Not arrogant. Simply intent on seizing what he wanted, what she had offered.

He peeled the small straps of her sundress down her shoulders and freed her arms. Now she was bare to the waist.

She saw the muscles in his throat ripple as he swallowed. "You're beautiful, Layla."

Suddenly, she was ravenous for him. "There's a zipper in the back," she whispered. "Hurry."

His smile was crooked. "What's your rush?"

"It's been a very long time since I've enjoyed... *this*."

The grin faded. "I'll bet I've got you beat. Almost two years. My ex slept around during our separation. I still felt married."

"And since February?"

He shrugged, his jawline rigid. "Nobody. I've been a mess, Layla. Are you sure you want to get involved with a guy who screwed up his life?"

She put her hands on his biceps, loving the feel of his muscles. "We're not getting involved," she said, finding the courage to stare into his eyes. "We're living in the moment. I can't say I have much experience with that way of thinking. I'm wound pretty tight. But for you, I'll make an exception."

Clearly, she had struck the right tone with her lighthearted teasing. Joshua's gorgeous smile returned, the wattage melting her body into a pool of feminine lust.

"I'm flattered," he muttered, bending to lick the tips of her breasts.

Holy hell. Layla arched her back, trying desperately to get closer. Somehow, he reached beneath her and dealt with the zipper. Soon he had her naked except for her tiny undies. Even though the sun was almost gone, she could feel its warmth on her skin.

Or maybe she was simply hyped up on the erotic way Joshua played with her body. He seemed fascinated with her flat belly, her navel, her thighs. When he touched her *there*, she bit her bottom lip to keep from begging.

For a man who professed to be celibate in recent days, he was remarkably patient.

When she said as much—muttering her disgruntlement—Joshua threw back his head and laughed uproariously.

"I wasn't trying to be funny. You're still dressed," she wailed, aggrieved.

Lightning flashed in his eyes, turning the placid blue to stormy skies. "I don't have much faith in my control once I get inside you, Layla. At least not the first time. I wanted the foreplay to be good for you, for me."

She dragged his head down. "We can always do the foreplay afterward."

Though she initiated the kiss, Joshua took control pretty damn fast. His tongue mated with hers. He sucked gently.

Heated need made her limbs heavy. Her sex throbbed with an insistent ache that begged to be assuaged. Layla felt a sudden dollop of unease. Why was she so susceptible to this man? Were nostalgia and hormones to blame?

And then the kiss deepened, eliminating any impulse on her part to think rationally.

There was no explanation for what was happening. None that made sense.

She wanted Joshua Banks more than she wanted her next breath.

He rolled away from her, panting. She watched as he extracted a square packet from his wallet and then unzipped his jeans. When he pulled his erect sex from his snug navy knit boxers, she sucked in a sharp breath.

Thankfully, Joshua didn't seem to notice. He positioned the condom and returned to her, settling between her legs. His gaze was hooded. "You ready?"

"Yes." The word was barely audible.

Joshua entered her with one powerful thrust. The clouds and treetops cartwheeled behind her eyelids as she squeezed her eyes shut and gave in to the sheer carnality of the moment. He was careful with her, tender even. But this was raw sex. No hearts and flowers. Just a man and a woman battling a powerful need.

They clung to each other on the sun-warmed quilt, struggling for more depth, more thrust, more everything.

She nipped his bottom lip with sharp teeth. "Don't hold back, Josh. I want it all."

The groan that ripped from somewhere deep inside him echoed the madness she felt. Desperation was a tangible cloud surrounding them. She inhaled his scent, felt the odd paradox of security and exhilaration.

He came first, but only seconds before she lost her mind. The orgasm was blissful, perfect, draining and energizing in equal measures.

In the aftermath, he kissed her forehead, then shifted slightly to give her room to breathe. But they were still connected. He was inside her, mostly still erect. Tantalizingly ready for round two.

At last, she found her voice. "Wow…"

He ran his thumb along her bottom lip. "Ditto…"

"Josh?" The shortened version of his name slipped out. It was what she had called him when they were kids.

"Yeah?"

"What was that we just did?"

"If you don't know, I must have done it wrong."

The humorous, self-deprecating words didn't match the solemn look in his eyes. It was hard to meet those eyes. They saw too much, perhaps. For the first time in her life, Layla had just indulged in the equivalent of a bar pickup. A one-night stand.

To a control freak, this total lapse of judgment on her part was terrifying.

"We're practically strangers," she whispered.

"Are we?" Joshua's face closed up. He rolled to his feet, straightened his clothing and turned his back so she could do the same.

When they were both dressed, she stood up, too. "I need help with my zipper," she muttered.

She presented her back to her lover and shivered when his warm fingers brushed her spine.

It took courage to turn around and face him. "I'm sorry," she said.

Now his scowl was fierce. He folded his arms across his chest. "For what?"

She shrugged, feeling small and uncertain and insecure. "I used you for sexual satisfaction."

Those blue eyes threatened to burn her. "I see. And you think I did the same?"

"Didn't you?" She wanted badly to hear him say otherwise, but the evidence was hard to discount.

In the time it took a breeze to ruffle the new leaves overhead, every emotion disappeared from his face. "I'll take you home."

"Wait," she said. "Don't be mad. I'm just trying to understand."

"It was sex," he said flatly. "Pretty incredible sex. But if it's spooked you this badly, it was clearly a mistake."

"I'm not spooked," she said quickly.

Finally, a giant sigh lifted his chest. One corner

of his mouth quirked in an almost smile. He unfolded his arms and slid his hands beneath her hair, cupping her neck. He bent his head to stare into her eyes. "Could have fooled me. Relax, Layla. We enjoyed each other. Is that so terrible?"

"I am *not* a sex maniac."

Now he chuckled. He brushed his lips over hers. "I wouldn't complain if you were. This was a hell of a way to break my fast."

"Why with me?" The words burst from her lips.

"Are you asking me to explain sexual attraction?"

She rested her cheek against his chest. "I've never had sex with someone just for the heck of it. It's always been part of a relationship."

"Are you proposing?" he asked, deadpan.

"Stop trying to make me feel dumb." She punched his shoulder.

He slid his fingers through her hair. "Can't we just enjoy ourselves? Does there have to be an answer for everything?"

She stared at him for the longest time, trying to read the mix of expressions on his face. If she didn't know better, she would think he was as surprised as she was by the connection between them.

"Why don't you kiss me again?" she said. "To see if it was a fluke."

"*It* what?" He moved closer, his big frame dwarfing hers.

Sharing the same air made it hard to breathe. "The spark," she croaked. "The fire."

That arrogant masculine grin was back. "I like the way you think." He held her head and tipped it the direction he needed, settling on the exact slant to cover her mouth with his and make them both groan with pleasure.

Layla wrapped one leg around his thigh. It was good. So good. Surely this was more than deprivation making her feel like she was melting into a puddle. She was ridiculously aroused. Clinging. Desperate.

She spared a half second to wonder who this woman was. She wasn't a version of Layla anyone would recognize.

Suddenly, Joshua scooped her into his arms and strode toward the vehicle. Layla was disappointed. She wasn't ready to go home.

But her companion had other ideas. He set her on the hood of the sports car. The metal was warm from the sun, but not uncomfortably hot.

The next round of kissing was more intense. Joshua moved between her legs, shimmying her skirt up her thighs. Getting close. And closer still.

His erection, covered in thick denim, felt good pressed against her center. When he rocked back and forth, Layla's fingernails dug into his forearms. "Please," she muttered. "Please tell me that wasn't your only condom."

Instead of answering, he growled low in his throat. His big hands cupped her butt and he lifted her into his thrusts. Like two teenagers fooling around, they tried to climb inside each other's skin.

Joshua's chest heaved with the force of his labored breathing. "Can't let go," he said.

"You have to. Right now. Please. I need you, but not without protection."

On the surface, she sounded logical and forthright. Thank goodness he couldn't see inside her confused brain. If he had told her the first condom was the only one, she might have rolled the dice and taken her chances. *That* was how much she wanted him.

"Ten seconds," he promised. He left her and jerked open the car door. She watched through the windshield as he rummaged in the glove box. His jawline was granite. His hair was tousled, his cheekbones flushed.

She rested her bare feet on the slick hood, trying not to slide off.

When he came back to her, he took care of business quickly and touched her undies. "Now?" he asked gruffly.

All she could do was nod.

Joshua didn't even bother removing her panties. He simply pushed them to one side and entered her with a raw, powerful surge that dried her throat and brought emotion to the fore. She didn't want that. All she wanted was sex.

But it was impossible not to feel things. Because she didn't know how to trust this madness, she shoved all those messy, warm responses away, concentrating on the carnal present.

Joshua Banks was good in bed. Or maybe not.

Who knew? But he was a heck of a lover in the great outdoors.

Now she linked her ankles at his back. She dragged his head closer so she could kiss him wildly. "Don't stop," she panted. "Don't ever stop."

His shoulders shook with laughter, but his eyes glittered with hunger. "I'd like to oblige, Layla, but you rev me up too damn fast."

His words were prophetic. Suddenly, he pounded into her feverishly. The hood of his car might never be the same. He moaned her name as he found his release. At the last instant, he shifted to one side and thumbed her center.

She shuddered and cried out his name as she hit the peak and tumbled over the other side.

Six

Joshua could hear his heart beating inside his ears. His knees were bruised from thumping against the side of the car. And somehow, despite their location beneath a broad, expansive Texas sky, he was starved of oxygen.

The woman in his arms stirred. "Sweet heaven."

There was no blasphemy in her awed whisper. He would have uttered words of agreement, but his tongue was thick in his mouth.

Truth be told, Joshua was as shaken as his partner. For months, he had found release with a hand job in the shower. His life had been in too much turmoil for anything else. And even after the divorce was final, he'd had a vague distaste for the idea of picking up a strange woman in a bar.

He might have done that a few times in his twenties, but he was older now. Wiser. Good Lord, he hoped he was wiser. Surely he should have something to show for a marriage that imploded. As it was, he had plenty of regrets.

The sex with Layla had been volcanic. Feelings and emotions he had ignored forever suddenly bubbled to the surface. Why had he never dated Layla? She was only a year younger than he was.

But when he still lived in Royal, she hadn't really been on his radar. She was just the funny, spunky kid who ran around with Jordan and him when they were all in middle school and early high school. Thinking of his brother brought up another sore point. What if Layla had been thinking of *Jordan* when she was having sex with Joshua?

His stomach curled. She might have done that without even realizing what she was doing. Joshua was damned if he would be a stand-in for his more gregarious sibling.

Only once had the twins fixated on the same girl. It had been eleventh grade. They both wanted to ask Tiffany Tarwater to the prom. Things had gotten ugly. After that, they made a pact. No fighting over females. Ever.

Suddenly, he realized Layla was stroking the back of his neck. His body tightened as another wave of arousal—one that had merely been simmering below the surface—seized him. His throat dried.

He had taken her like a savage. Never before in his life had he experienced more desperation, or more lust. Though he was shocked at himself, the woman in his arms wasn't trying to get away, so maybe all was not lost. Carefully, he lifted her into a seated position.

Her skin was warm and silky, her golden tresses a tangled mess. He buried his face against her bare shoulder, wanting to say something, but finding himself mute.

Layla combed through his hair with gentle fingers.

Separating their bodies was an actual physical pain. After he got rid of the condom and straightened his clothes, he turned around to find Layla looking at him.

What was that expression he saw in her beautiful eyes?

Try as he might, he couldn't come up with a single word.

Layla cocked her head, still staring into his soul… or so it seemed. "Your ex-wife is an idiot," she said calmly.

He felt his face flush. The implied compliment was reassuring, but still… "I don't want to talk about my ex," he said bluntly.

Layla grimaced. "Understandable."

"I suppose I should take you home," he said, try-ing—after the fact—to act like a gentleman.

His lover nodded slowly. "I suppose."

When he helped her stand, she wobbled. They both laughed.

Layla's smile was wistful, but at least it was a smile.

He retrieved the quilt along with the remnants of their picnic supper and followed her to the car. When he would have started the engine, Layla put her hand on his arm. "That was incredible," she said softly. "But I'm not sure where we go from here."

He sensed her need for clarification. But hell, he was befuddled. "What do you mean?" he asked, mostly to stall for time.

One slender shoulder lifted and fell in a feminine shrug. "You're having a personal crisis of identity. You have no idea if you're even going to stay in Royal. And my whole family is embroiled in a busi-ness emergency. Neither of us is in a healthy place to start a relationship."

Then she blushed. "Or maybe that wasn't what you had in mind."

He tried to frame a response. Honestly? He wasn't looking for a relationship at all. But his body appar-ently had a different agenda. The thought of leaving the lovely Layla free and unattached didn't sit well.

"All I know is that I want to see you again."

She blinked. Maybe the staccato, machine-gun words had shocked her.

"Ditto," she said. "But this week is packed."

"Can you find time for me? For us?"

Pink bloomed on her cheekbones. "I'll try."

"Fair enough."

This time when he started the engine, she didn't stop him.

The journey back to town was slower and almost as silent as the earlier trip when his passenger had been asleep beside him. He couldn't glean much from her expression. Her face was turned away from him as she stared out the side window, apparently fascinated by the fields of Indian paintbrush.

The bluebonnets were long gone. The winter had been mild, and they bloomed early. At the time, Joshua had still been in Dallas, closed up in his office by day and in his sterile apartment by night.

Why had he ever believed a corporate job was for him? He knew a hell of a lot about the oil industry, and he had been a damned good project manager, but the work hadn't satisfied an ache in his gut.

What had he been missing? Maybe everything.

At the Grandin ranch house, he parked in front of the steps and turned to face the woman who had bewitched him. He leaned forward and kissed her long and deep, though he kept his passion reined in for obvious reasons.

When he pulled back, Layla's pink lips were puffy. She touched his cheek. "It was a good picnic," she said solemnly. "I'm glad we cleared the air."

For a moment, he had forgotten all about the

Jordan/Joshua twin swap. Embarrassment cramped his stomach. "I'm really sorry about the bait and switch. I should have said no to my brother."

Layla got out and stared at him over the top of the car as he exited as well. "But think what we might have missed." Her mischievous smile brought his hunger roaring back.

He rounded the car and pulled her into the shadows, away from the illumination of the porch lights. "We'll figure this out," he promised.

"Maybe." She leaned her head against his shoulder. "Don't make promises you can't keep. We've both failed at important relationships. We're not sure what we want. Life is complicated."

The more negatives she threw at him, the stronger his impulse to convince her.

But now was not the time. "We've always been friends," he said, his tone mild. "We still are."

"True." She patted his chest with two hands. "I'll keep in touch. You, too. Maybe we can squeeze in dinner or a movie."

"I'd rather be alone with you."

Her eyes gleamed in the half dark. "Naughty, Mr. Banks."

"My brother isn't the only one who knows how to flirt."

"I'm sorry if my comparison was hurtful. I didn't mean it that way."

He made himself let her go. "You didn't hurt anything. At least not in a bad way. Some things hurt really, really *good*."

This time, she laughed. "And on that note, I'll say good-night."

"See you soon," he said. Was it a promise or a wish?

He watched as she climbed the stairs. On the top step, she turned and waved. "Good night, Josh."

Hearing her shorten his name gave him a funny feeling inside. Few people called him that anymore. But Layla had…once upon a time.

Back at the hotel, all he wanted to do was shower, flip channels for an hour or two and crash. But his brother was waiting for him in the hotel lobby.

Jordan jumped to his feet, his expression disgruntled. "Where in the heck have you been? You just got back into town. Surely your social life hasn't heated up that fast."

Joshua counted to ten. No point in taking his brother's taunting seriously. "As a matter of fact, I was out with Layla. I told her about our little stunt."

"Was she mad?"

"Actually, she was pretty cool about it."

"Ah…"

"What does that mean?"

"I'm guessing she was disappointed that it wasn't me."

"Sure didn't seem that way." Joshua glared at his twin. "Any crush Layla Grandin had on you is so far in the past nobody has the forwarding address."

"Very funny."

Joshua shoved his hands in his pockets. "Why are you here?"

"Dad wants you to come out to the ranch. So we can all talk."

"I see." Joshua couldn't decide if this overture was a plus or a minus. "Did you already tell him my divorce is finalized?"

"I had to. Otherwise, he might have thought she was here with you."

"Perish the thought."

"Indeed." Jordan ran a hand through his hair. "So you'll come?"

"Tell him I'll head out that way before lunch tomorrow. But I'm keeping the hotel room for now. I've got a lot to think about, and I need some space to decide my next move."

"Nothing to decide. You're back. End of story."

Actually, there was plenty more to the story, but Joshua wasn't keen to get into an argument now. "Thanks for coming, Jordan. I'll see you both in the morning."

They hugged, and with a jaunty wave, Jordan headed toward the exit.

Joshua made it to his room and crashed facedown on the bed. Unfortunately, he was far from being sleepy. He was hyped up on great sex and a million questions about his future. Coming home to Royal had been a gut-level impulse. Like an animal seeking shelter in its den, Joshua had wanted a place to hide out while he made plans.

But that was the trouble with hiding from reality. A man had only himself to blame when things went sideways.

The future was murky.

The morning after her picnic with Josh, Layla found herself energized and confused. Her family was still in disaster mode. Vic was still heir to the throne. But Layla was suddenly far more interested in her own personal life than anything about the ranch.

Maybe she was practicing avoidance. Or maybe Joshua Banks was impossible to ignore. The man was hot, sexy and too damn charming for his own good.

Her grandmother unwittingly offered a distraction. At lunchtime, she and Layla ended up in the kitchen together. While the housekeeper put together the sandwiches they had requested, Miriam leaned in and whispered, "Can we eat on the veranda out back? I need to ask you something. In private."

"Sure, Grammy." Layla was concerned. Her widowed grandmother didn't look good. She had deep shadows beneath her eyes as if she hadn't been sleeping well. But that was normal, right? The elderly woman had lost her husband. She was in mourning.

Once the two of them were settled on the wide screened-in porch overlooking the flower garden,

Miriam didn't start eating right away. Her hands twisted in her lap, plucking at the folds of her faded cotton *housecoat*. Although Miriam loved to dress up and had a closet full of fashionable clothing, here at the ranch house on a weekday she reverted to the relaxed workaday style of her mother and her mother's mother.

"What is it, Grammy?" Layla asked. "What's going on? And FYI, you really need to eat something. I don't want you getting sick."

Miriam smiled. "You're a peach, baby girl. Don't you worry about me. But here's the thing." She glanced around to make sure no one was close, and then she lowered her voice. "Will you drive me to the lawyer's office? I made an appointment for 1:30. But I don't want anyone else in the family to know."

"How are we supposed to pull that off?"

"Your father is out riding the range with his foreman. Bethany flew to Houston this morning with several friends for some fashion show. It's only Chelsea, Vic and Morgan we have to dodge."

"Only?"

"We can do it." Miriam didn't offer any further details. Instead, she bit into her sandwich and managed to finish half of it.

As they ate, Layla pondered the situation. Her grandmother was obviously being secretive. Although Layla's father was acting as if he had inherited the ranch outright, on paper he and Miriam were co-owners until his mother's death. So Miriam had as much right as anyone to meet with the family lawyers.

"I think this is the day that Vic and Morgan play doubles tennis at the Cattleman's Club," Layla said. "If I can make sure Chelsea isn't around, you and I should be able to get away with no one the wiser."

"And when we come home," her grandmother said, "we'll just say we went shopping." Her face lit up as if the small subterfuge tickled her.

"Sure," Layla said. "Whatever you want." Her grandmother meant the world to her. Layla would do anything to make Grammy happy, though it might be a very long time until Miriam Grandin regained her joie de vivre. Losing a spouse after so many years was a terrible blow.

As it turned out, Chelsea was spending the afternoon with a friend who had a new baby. So no one was around to see Layla and Miriam, both nicely dressed, walk down the front steps and get into Layla's Mini Cooper. Her father had poked fun at her for buying such a small, whimsical car, but Layla liked it.

At the lawyer's office, the two women had to wait only six or seven minutes in the lobby before they were ushered into the same room where the extended family had met to discuss the oil rights situation. Though Layla was prepared to step in if necessary, her grandmother handled herself with poise and determination.

She eyed the lawyer sternly. "I am here on a private matter. Do I have your word that what we discuss is confidential?"

The man's expression was affronted. "I assure you, Mrs. Grandin, I hold myself to a high ethical standard."

Miriam made a sound suspiciously like a snort. As she sat down in the chair closest to the man's broad cherry desk, she opened her 1960s' era handbag and pulled out a three-by-five leather-bound journal. The small book was maybe half an inch thick.

She paused, perhaps for dramatic effect. "I found one of my husband's diaries. More than one, actually, but this is the pertinent time period. I always knew he hid these, but I never bothered to look for them. My husband was one hundred percent faithful to our marriage. Other than that, his little secrets didn't really concern me."

She handed the tiny book to Layla, who had taken a seat as well. "I've marked the spot with a sticky note. Please read it aloud."

Layla eyed the lawyer and vice versa. Then she took a deep breath. The ink was faded. Grandy's spidery handwriting was immediately recognizable. This particular entry had been recorded more than three decades earlier.

She could almost hear his voice…

Augustus and I did what we had to do today. We signed over the oil rights on the adjoining ranches to protect Daniel. The boy is thriving in Paris. No need for him to come home and deal with a mess.

We put the rights in this Cynthia person's name and warned her not to claim anything until the baby was grown. I think she knows we have the money and the clout to make her life a misery if she tries any funny business.

Layla's nerveless fingers dropped the book in her lap. "My God, it's true."

Even the lawyer went pale.

Miriam straightened her spine. "Those two old men have caused untold damage with this stunt."

Layla stared at her grandmother. "We have to tell Daddy. And everyone else."

"No. We don't." Color stained the old woman's cheeks. "Cynthia and her daughter are dead. It's possible Heath Thurston fabricated a document based on rumors he'd heard from his mother. Who knows if Daniel was really Ashley's father? Victor has hired an investigator. For now, we let things run their course." She gave the poor lawyer a regal glare. "I wanted you to know the truth, so you can be prepared. We may be able to stonewall Thurston and buy ourselves some time."

The lawyer cleared his throat. "I can't be involved in anything illegal, Mrs. Grandin. Surely you know that."

Miriam stood, her chest heaving with rapid breaths. "I won't let my family's legacy be destroyed. That's all you need to know."

Layla saw the dampness on her grandmother's

brow and the way her pupils dilated. "We can meet here again if we need to, but, Grammy, I think I should take you home."

Suddenly, Miriam wobbled and collapsed to the floor.

Layla's heart jumped out of her chest. "Call 911," she yelled at the lawyer. She barely heard the man's words on the phone as she knelt beside her grandmother. The old woman's face was paper white.

For a few moments, Layla was terrified she had lost a second grandparent. But finally, she located a shallow pulse in her grandmother's wrist.

The next thirty minutes were a blur. Hearing sirens in the distance. Putting wet paper towels on her grandmother's forehead. Rubbing her frail arms.

As soon as the EMTs arrived, they took over with a minimum of fuss. They spent several minutes stabilizing Miriam and then lifted her carefully onto a stretcher. Fortunately, the law office was on the ground floor.

Layla felt her heart crack as she watched the stretcher being loaded in the back of the emergency vehicle. Grammy looked so frail and ill.

"I'd like to ride there with her," Layla said, preparing to climb in.

The young female medic shook her head, though there was sympathy in her eyes. "Sorry, Ms. Grandin. It's not allowed. The area is small, and we have to be able to work on your grandmother. You're welcome to meet us at the emergency room."

Seconds later, the truck sped off, sirens blazing.

Layla didn't know what to do. Her mother was out of town. Her father was riding on the far reaches of the ranch where cell service was spotty. And besides, Grammy had wanted this outing to be a secret.

Layla stood on the street corner, frozen.

Joshua was headed back to town after a not-so-successful visit to the ranch where he had grown up. As he made the turn toward his hotel, he saw Layla standing in front of a lawyer's office. She looked upset. Immediately, he pulled into a parking spot at the curb and jumped out.

"Layla. What's wrong? Are you hurt?"

She turned her head and stared at him blankly. Her face, even her lips, were pale. When he put his arms around her, she burst into tears.

It took him several minutes to drag the story from her. "I have to go to the emergency room," she said, looking frantic.

"You're in no shape to get behind the wheel. I'll take you."

He bundled her into the car and drove ten miles above the speed limit to Royal Memorial Hospital. Layla sat, huddled into herself, and closed her eyes. When they arrived, the state-of-the-art medical center was a hive of activity.

Layla tried to get him to drop her off at the door and leave, but Joshua wasn't about to do that. "They won't let you go back in Emergency. Not until they've fully evaluated her. I'll sit with you in the waiting room."

Joshua handed off his keys to the valet parking attendant, helped Layla out of the car and stuck with her.

No matter how upscale the hospital and how bright the paint and the floor coverings, all waiting rooms were essentially the same. Filled with antiseptic smells, the aura of fear and grief and an overwhelming sense of life and death.

Layla checked in at the desk only to be told that her grandmother hadn't been admitted yet. She looked up at Joshua, her brow creased with worry. "She's eighty-eight years old. Surely they won't send her home."

"They'll do whatever is best for her, I'm sure. Come sit down."

He tried to distract her with conversation, but to no avail.

At one point, Layla jumped to her feet and paced. "It's my fault."

"How?" He frowned, seeing her frantic state and unable to help her.

"Grammy wanted me to take her to the lawyer's office for a private meeting. She didn't want the rest of the family to know. So I said I would, but…"

"But what?"

Layla chewed her lip. "She collapsed while we were there."

"Do you want to tell me what was going on?"

"Maybe. But not now."

"Okay." He took her wrist as she made another circuit in his direction. "Sit, Layla. You're going to need to be strong to help your grandmother. Right now, you're wearing yourself out."

To his relief, Layla finally collapsed into the space beside him. It was a two-person love seat, no inconvenient metal bar in the middle. He slid an arm around her shoulders. "Breathe," he said. "Everything is going to be okay."

Layla half turned and glared at him. "You don't know that. People *die.*"

Tears spilled from those blue eyes that made him weak in the knees. He pulled her closer. "Aw, hell, Layla. Don't do this. I can handle anything but you falling apart."

She had always been one of the strongest females he knew. To be honest, he and Jordan hadn't merely *tolerated* her presence when they were younger, they had *enjoyed* having her around.

Of course, being teenage boys, they never articulated those feelings.

Without warning, all the fire left her. She leaned into his embrace, not saying another word. But the slow tears didn't stop. Each one dug a little knife into his heart.

She looked even more beautiful than usual wearing a black pencil skirt, a sleeveless ivory silk blouse tucked in at the waist and low heels that matched the skirt. Her hair was pulled back into a sleek, sophisticated ponytail.

He stroked the nape of her neck and waited with her, wondering what he was doing with this woman in this spot. He'd done a lot of soul searching after he dropped her off last night. The negative column was staggering.

First of all, there was the matter of her crush on Jordan. Josh looked *exactly* like his twin. There was a decent chance that Layla was unconsciously using Joshua as a stand-in for the guy she really wanted. It was a tough pill to swallow, but Josh had to at least consider the possibility.

Second, Layla's family was in crisis mode. She hadn't opened up to him yet about the specifics, but it was something serious enough to involve the whole clan. Which meant Layla needed to be there for her parents, her siblings and, of course, her newly widowed grandmother.

Then there was the matter of Joshua himself. It was hard to be confident about a new relationship when he had so badly botched his marriage. It wouldn't be fair to any woman to get involved until he knew what he wanted out of life.

Did he want to work with his father and Jordan? Did he want to go somewhere else—create a new life on his own terms? Houston was great. The museums, the art, the music. The sporting events. He had buddies in Houston. It would be a perfect place to relocate, and the job market was solid.

But then there was Royal. This quirky town with its history and its roots and its way of pulling a guy back home. Deep down, he felt like this was where he was supposed to be. But doing what? His father and Jordan didn't really *need* him. Joshua wanted to make his own mark in the world.

If he was smart, he would put the brakes on this thing with Layla.

Yet as good and sensible as his plan sounded, he couldn't work up any enthusiasm at all for any of the choices that didn't involve her.

She made him shudder…made him yearn. In ways that made him question why he had ever thought Becky was the one.

He wasn't stupid. He knew that sexual attraction could burn hot and bright and then ultimately flame out and turn to ash…or merely cool off gradually.

He'd had enough girlfriends over the years to realize that.

Was he kidding himself to think Layla was different? There was *something* between them, something almost irresistible. Lust? He'd known lust before. He was a guy, after all. And maybe the only difference with Layla was that they shared a past as adolescents.

But he couldn't convince himself that was it. Even now, in a setting entirely nonconducive to sexual thoughts, he knew he wanted her. He felt possessive and protective. Most of all, he trembled with the need to make love to her.

Was that normal? Was he having some kind of early midlife crisis?

She stirred in his embrace, sitting up straight and rubbing her face. "Talk to me," she said. "I can't stand this waiting. Tell me about your day. Or anything."

He nodded. "Well, I went out to the ranch to see my father this morning."

"Is this the first time since you've been back in Royal?"

"Yes. I needed a few days to get my thoughts settled."

"How did it go?"

He hesitated. "Not like I thought it would. Jordan says Dad will take me back in a heartbeat, but I don't think it's that simple."

"Oh? Why not?"

He shrugged. "Just a gut feeling. He wants me to admit he was right and I was wrong. He never liked Becky and didn't want me to marry her."

"So you think he wants you to eat crow?"

"Yeah…"

"And will you?" She looked at him curiously, not judging.

"I don't mind admitting I was wrong. But I'm not sure my being back at the ranch permanently is such a good idea. Dad and Jordan have things under control. I might feel like a third wheel."

"But don't you own a share of the property?"

"I do. I've been a silent partner since I moved to Dallas."

Layla opened her mouth to say something but was interrupted when a scrubs-clad doctor pushed through the swinging doors.

"Ms. Grandin? Ms. Layla Grandin?"

Seven

Layla held Josh's hand in a death grip as she crossed the room. His strong arm curled around her shoulders, and his warm fingers twined with hers. That physical support was the only thing keeping her grounded at the moment.

Desperately, she searched the doctor's face. Was there some patient-care course in med school that taught them how to keep all expression under wraps?

"How is she?" Layla asked, her throat tight with fear.

The doc gave her an impersonal half smile. "Mrs. Grandin is stable. I've spoken with her at length. She thinks she may have forgotten to take her medication this morning. Consequently, her blood pressure bottomed out. Stress is also a factor. In addition, she hasn't been eating and drinking properly since her husband died. We're going to keep her a couple of days for observation. I've expressed to her how vital it is to care for her body while her heart heals."

That last poetic turn of phrase made Layla rethink her opinion of the young doctor. "Thank you," she said.

"Does she have anyone to stay with her when she goes home?"

"Oh, yes. Plenty of us. Don't worry, Doctor. We'll wait on her hand and foot—I promise."

When the man returned the way he had come, Layla looked up at her rescuer. His hair was disheveled. He probably needed a haircut. But the thing that stood out most in this moment was Josh's absolute strength of character. She *knew* she could depend on him. Even before today—when he had dropped everything he was doing and stepped in to care for her—she understood that about his code of conduct. "Thanks," she said. "I was a wreck, but I'm okay now. You can go."

He frowned at her. "If I'm not mistaken, you'll need a ride back to your car. Or better yet, I'll take you straight home, and someone can pick up your car later. It's in the wrong direction."

Layla hated admitting he was right. Though she was grateful to him, she didn't want to feel obligated to anyone, much less Josh. Not after he had seen her naked. There were too many unanswered questions for her to be completely sanguine about his presence at the hospital.

"That would be helpful," she said grudgingly.

Josh kissed the tip of her nose. "That hurt, didn't it? Admitting you needed help?"

She scowled. "And your point?"

"Sometimes it's nice to let someone take care of you."

Layla felt herself leaning into him, drowning in blue eyes that promised all sorts of delicious delights. "I don't need a man to look after me." She whispered the words automatically, trying to ignore the warmth spreading in her chest. The warmth Josh had put there with his kindness.

Yet, *kind* wasn't the adjective she should have used. There was banked fire in his eyes, as if the sexual connection between them was on the back burner but ready to burst into flame. The intensity of that gaze made it hard to breathe for a moment.

Fortunately for her, a nurse approached them. "Mrs. Grandin is being admitted right now. She'll be in room 317. If you want to wait for her up there, it shouldn't be long."

"Thank you," Layla said. She turned to Joshua again. "Seriously. You don't have to stay. I'm going to text my siblings. They'll all be showing up soon. And my father, too. Somebody will take me back to get my car eventually."

A second ticked by. Then five more. Joshua sighed. "I'd like to stay. When someone else in your family takes a turn, you could go back to the hotel with me and relax. Then maybe dinner in the hotel dining room. Or even room service?"

Layla searched his face. "Is *relax* code for something?"

His grin was wry. "Only if you want it to be. My hotel is near the hospital. It saves you going out to the ranch. You could take a nap. Watch something on TV."

"Make love to my childhood friend?" Rarely was she so sexually direct, but Josh might not be sticking around Royal.

He blinked. "I'm at your disposal, Ms. Grandin."

The next hour passed quickly. When they went upstairs, Josh insisted on remaining in a nearby waiting room across the hall while Layla helped get her grandmother settled.

Not long after that, Chelsea, Vic and Morgan arrived. When a nurse came to check the patient's vitals, the siblings stepped out in the hall and sketched out a quick schedule of who would sit with Miriam.

Chelsea insisted on taking first shift. "You need some rest, Layla. You look terrible. Seeing Grammy collapse must have been scary as hell."

"It was," Layla sighed.

Vic and Morgan chimed in, too. "We've got this," Vic said. "And Dad will be on his way later. Take the rest of the day for yourself. Come back in the morning."

Layla allowed herself to be persuaded. All the

adrenaline had winnowed away, leaving her shaky and exhausted. After bidding her grandmother good-bye, she found Josh in the waiting room. "I'm ready," she said.

Despite the events of the day, she drew strength from his solid presence. But his hand on her elbow as they stood in the elevator made her thoughts go in a different direction. Her skin warmed and tingled where his fingers touched her.

Outside, as they waited for the valet, she decided to go for what she wanted. "Would you mind taking me to the ranch first? I can pack a bag, and then I'll probably book a room at the hotel, too. So I'll be on hand until Grammy is released."

Josh stared at her, eyes narrowed. "I like most of that plan. But there's no need for a second room. You're more than welcome to stay with me. In fact, I'll be pissed if you don't. I want to be with you, Layla."

His plain speaking touched something deep in a corner of her psyche that she seldom poked at. Her whole life she had felt invisible much of the time. Chelsea was the oldest. Morgan the youngest. Vic the beloved only boy.

Layla had gotten lost in the crowd.

Now here was Josh. Putting her first. Telling her how much he wanted her.

Was this more than physical attraction, or was she letting herself be blinded by lust dressed up as caring and connection?

On the drive to the ranch, they barely spoke.

"I'll stay in the car," Josh said as they pulled up in front.

It wouldn't have mattered. No one was home but the housekeeping staff. "Okay," she said. "It won't take me long to grab what I need." Less than twenty-four hours ago, Layla had been kissing Josh in the shadows of the front porch. Now Grammy was ill, Layla was going to spend the night in Josh's hotel room and Layla now knew for certain that Grandy and Augustus Lattimore had signed away the oil rights to both ranches.

The world didn't make sense anymore.

In her closet, she stood on her tiptoes and pulled down a medium-sized suitcase. She was an experienced traveler, so packing wasn't a problem. She would mostly need comfortable clothes for sitting in a hospital room.

Toiletries were next. A few personal items. The only thing that stumped her was what to wear in bed. It had been a long time since she had dressed up for a man at night. Though she enjoyed expensive lingerie, it felt naughty to deliberately pack things she knew Josh would enjoy. Maybe for that exact reason, she folded two beautiful gowns with matching silky robes and tucked them into her bag.

By the time she made it out to the porch and re-locked the front door, Josh surprised her by showing up to carry her bag down the stairs. "It's heavy," he said when she protested.

Her nerves grew as they got closer to the hotel. Josh reached over and patted her arm. "Quit panicking. We won't do anything you don't want to do."

"That's the trouble," she said morosely. "I want to do *everything* with you."

Josh's chuckle and smug smile told her he knew exactly what was on her mind.

She kept in touch with her family via a group text. Grammy was feeling much better. She was getting IV fluids and had eaten a small dinner.

Because Josh was already a guest at the hotel, there was no need to visit the front desk. Layla felt as if every set of eyes in the lobby followed them when they stepped into the elevator. She couldn't look at herself in the mirrored walls as the numbers lit up one by one.

What was she doing? To say she was choosing to spend the night in Josh's room because it was convenient and economical was a ridiculous stretch when it came to rationalization. She needed to be honest with herself. This was 99 percent about sex. Hot, sweaty, amazing sex.

She lost her nerve when Josh opened his door and stepped back for her to enter. Layla had been hoping he had a suite. But he didn't. Although the room was very large and luxurious—even with a comfy sitting area—there was no escaping the fact that the enormous king-size bed dominated the space.

Josh set her suitcase just outside the bathroom door and tossed his keys on the dresser. "So what will it be, Layla? Room service, or dinner out?" His cocky, sexy grin told her he knew she was not as confident as she appeared.

There was really no question. She needed some breathing space. "Dinner out would be nice," she said primly.

Joshua nodded. "There's a new French bistro just around the corner. The concierge recommended it to me."

She cocked her head and stared at him. "You don't really strike me as a French bistro kind of guy."

His grin broadened, making her tummy quiver. "Maybe you don't know me as well as you think. Or then again, I might be expanding my horizons."

Layla didn't take the bait. In this battle of wits, he would probably win out, simply because it had been a very long, stressful day for her.

The outfit she had worn to the lawyer's office was suitable for dinner, so all she had to do was freshen up in the bathroom.

When it was Josh's turn, he grabbed a clean shirt and dress pants and took a five-minute shower. Though Layla seated herself on the opposite side of the room, it was impossible not to hear the water running and imagine what he looked like, his fit, muscular body wet and steamy.

The lump in her throat grew.

She couldn't look at him when he finally exited the bathroom. His scent, something lime and woodsy, invaded her senses, though to be fair, it was extremely subtle.

His damp hair was a darker blond than usual. It struck her suddenly that Joshua Banks was an incredibly handsome man. A stupid thought, probably. After all, she had known him for many years.

But now, seeing him all grown up—masculine and self-assured—she perceived him differently. Not as a preteen boy, or even an older adolescent. He had filled out. Matured. This man might still be her friend. Time would tell.

But he was also the lover she wanted.

They walked to the restaurant. It was a pleasant evening. People filled the streets. Music spilled from a nearby sports bar.

The bistro was just fancy enough to be romantic, but not so uppity that it seemed out of place in Royal. Layla was startled to hear Josh order an expensive bottle of wine in flawless French. When the waiter departed, she raised an eyebrow at the man sitting across from her. "Since when do you speak French?"

He shrugged. "College. Turns out I have a knack for languages. I do fairly well in Spanish, too. It came in handy when I was working for the energy company in Dallas. I traveled to Europe a couple of times a year."

"I see." She wanted to ask if his ex-wife traveled with him, but she couldn't bring herself to do it. It wasn't really any of her business—unless Josh somehow harbored unresolved feelings in that direction.

Just because his ex-spouse had not been the woman he thought she was didn't mean he hadn't cared about her. Maybe still did at some level.

After Richard's many deceptions, Layla had learned not to take everything at face value. People told you what they wanted you to believe. She needed to guard her heart and her emotions with Josh.

Great sex didn't always equal honesty.

Despite her misgivings, dinner was delightful. The food was incredible. The wine even better. And since neither of them was driving, they lingered and enjoyed the burgundy.

Josh told her funny stories about his job. She shared a few anecdotes about college and how she and Richard had met some years later.

Josh leaned back in his chair. "So are you going to tell me what's going on with the Grandin ranch?"

She wrinkled her nose. "I can share some but not all. A few things are need-to-know."

He nodded. "Fair enough. What's the deal?"

"Basically, it seems my uncle had an affair years ago. There was a child he didn't know about. Or so we've been told. If it's true, this same source claims that my grandfather and Augustus Lattimore signed over oil rights on both ranches to this woman to hold in trust until the baby grew up. But years later, the woman and her grown daughter died in a car accident."

"That's bizarre." Josh frowned. "So the oil rights were never activated?"

"Apparently not."

"Then the story is a lie?"

"We're not sure," Layla said carefully, trying not to think about the small journal with the incriminating evidence.

"Who is it?"

"Heath Thurston."

"I don't know him."

"Our whole family is going nuts. Daddy has hired an investigator."

"Makes sense. The claim will have to be substantiated."

"I guess. And if it's true..." She trailed off, feeling sick.

Josh reached across the table and squeezed her hand. His smile was encouraging. "Maybe it's not," he said. "Otherwise, why wouldn't the girl have claimed her inheritance when she turned twenty-one?"

Layla hadn't thought of that. A tiny flicker of hope stirred in her chest, despite what she had seen in the lawyer's office.

"Let's talk about something happier," she said.

Joshua obliged. Soon they were deep into a conversation about sports and possible pennants in the fall.

They had started on the dessert course—a decadent sponge cake with fresh raspberry sauce—when someone appeared beside their table. Layla looked up, thinking it was the waiter. Instead, their unexpected guest was a man about Josh's age. He had full, dark brown hair, dark eyes and thick eyebrows. He was as handsome and striking as the Banks brothers, but in a different way. His faded jeans and well-worn cowboy boots looked out of place in the fancy bistro.

It was *Heath Thurston*, the source of all her troubles. She had googled him after the funeral to be sure she knew what he looked like.

Josh, clearly not recognizing the man, stared at him. "May we help you?"

Thurston ignored Josh, choosing instead to focus all his attention on Layla. "Ms. Grandin? Layla Grandin?"

Unease slithered in her veins. "Yes."

A smile added charm to his serious face. "I'm Nolan Thurston."

Nolan… Her brain scrambled to keep up.

When Layla was silent, he elaborated. "My brother is Heath Thurston."

Layla shook her head slowly. "What is it with this town and twins? I can't believe you have the nerve to speak to me, especially in public."

Josh rose to his feet, tossing his cloth napkin on the table. "Get lost, Thurston."

Again, the man ignored Josh. When he addressed Layla again, his expression was conciliatory, his words couched in pleasant tones. "I wondered if you and I might have lunch together soon. You know. To talk things out. It's possible we can find some common ground before all of this gets blown out of proportion. And you could bring your sister Chelsea. She's the oldest...right? I've been told the two of you are close."

Layla stood as well, now flanked by two imposing men. "You're out of your mind," she said tersely. "No lunch. No dinner. No nothing. And stay away from my sister. Your brother is trying to destroy my family's livelihood."

Nolan's smile faded. "*Destroy* is a harsh word. Heath only wants what's fair. The oil rights are ours. Surely you can understand that. Take a step back and look at the situation unemotionally. What would you do if the situations were reversed?"

Eight

Josh had seen enough. Layla looked as if she might punch the guy. He lowered his voice and infused it with an audible threat. "Go. Away. Or I'll call the cops."

Nolan Thurston was a cool customer. He didn't seem at all rattled by Josh's posturing. "I'm not trying to cause trouble," he said. "Besides, what's it to you? I fail to see your connection to the matter. Unless you're a fiancé? Or a boyfriend?"

Josh ground his teeth, wishing he could wipe the smug smile off Thurston's face. "My relationship to Layla is none of your business."

Nolan shifted his gaze back to Layla. "Lawyers are expensive. I think it would be much more civilized if you and I—or any other of your siblings—could arbitrate a fair outcome that will satisfy us all."

Layla's spine stiffened. It almost seemed as if she grew two inches, like an Amazon in training. "To be honest, Mr. Thurston, I don't give a rat's ass about what might satisfy you and your avaricious brother. Your mother is gone. Your sister, too. Even if such an agreement ever existed—and I doubt that it did—any obligation ceased with your sister's passing."

Nolan scowled. "You don't know that. Sounds more like wishful thinking on your part. Have lunch with me. Soon. It's in everyone's best interests."

Layla placed her hands on her hips and lifted a haughty eyebrow. "Don't presume to know what's best for me or my family, Mr. Thurston. Grandins have worked that ranch for generations. We don't intend to let you and your brother ruin a single blade of grass."

Josh moved toward the man, fully prepared to usher him out of the restaurant by force, if necessary.

Fortunately, Thurston got the hint. He tossed his business card on the table and sighed. "Think about what I've said. Let me know if you change your mind. I'll be in touch."

When Nolan Thurston turned on his heel and walked rapidly out of the dining room, Layla sank into her chair as if her legs had collapsed. She rested her elbows on the table and put her head in her hands. "This has been the week from hell."

Josh didn't say a word. But he sat down quietly.

Thirty seconds later, Layla lifted her head and gave him a sheepish smile. "Present company excepted, of course. You've made my soap opera of a life bearable."

Her pink lips curved in a self-deprecating smile that sent a shiver down his spine. Suddenly, he was calculating how quickly he might persuade her to go back to the room. "You've had a rough go of it," he agreed. "I'm sorry Thurston interrupted our meal."

Layla poked at her now-soggy cake. "It's still good. Go ahead. Finish yours. Or I will." She laughed at him with her eyes. Her mouth was full of syrupy dessert.

Damn. How did she do that? One minute he wanted to comfort her. The next he was ready to strip her naked and take her right here on the table. To be honest, his impulses when he was around Layla were beginning to freak him out.

He didn't have a shrink on retainer, but if he did, this would have been a good time for some intensive *what-in-the-hell-are-you-thinking* therapy.

But that was the problem. He wasn't thinking. At all. He was only reacting and lusting and generally acting like the poor little sphere in a pinball machine, getting whacked from one side of the game to the other with flippers. Everyone who played knew the outcome of pinball was hard to predict. All the bells and whistles served as a distraction. The ball could end up anywhere.

He suddenly had an epiphany. He didn't need to

find all the answers today. Or even tomorrow. The important point was not to lose sight of the prize. One thing he knew for certain. Layla Grandin had skin in this game, whether she knew it or not. They had both been burned by love. They had that in common. But so had lots of people. Knowing what relationships *didn't* work was easy.

Predicting the future was a lot more difficult.

Layla swallowed the last bite of her cake and chased it with a final sip of wine. Then she sighed. "I'm stuffed. Do you want to go for a walk?"

Hell, no! He swallowed, praying he hadn't said those two words out loud. "Sure," he said, hoping his smile looked more genuine than it felt.

After he paid the check and they made it back out onto the street, his mood mellowed. The sun was down. A light breeze fluttered new leaves on the trees. He took Layla's hand in his. "You choose the path, Layla. I'll follow your lead."

They walked for half an hour, barely speaking. Enjoying the spring evening. He wondered if Layla was worrying about the Thurston brothers, but he didn't want to bring up a sore subject.

Eventually, their circuitous route took them back to the hotel. In the elevator, he tucked a strand of silky blond hair behind her ear. They were alone. No one to see when his thumb caressed her cheek.

Layla blushed. She searched his face, her long-lashed eyes locked on his. "Thank you," she said softly. "It's been a very long time since I've had somebody looking out for me. I may not *need* it, but that doesn't mean I don't appreciate everything you've done for me today. I'm not sure what would have happened if you hadn't shown up when you did."

"You would have thought of something."

"Maybe. But then again, I might have gotten behind the wheel to drive myself to the hospital. I was in shock, I think."

"Yeah."

In the room, he could see Layla's nerves. "I need to make a phone call," he said. "Why don't I do that downstairs to give you some privacy while you get ready for bed?"

The relief on her face almost made him laugh, but he didn't.

"Sounds good," she said breezily.

Though her words were light, her body language and the wariness in her gaze told him she wasn't sure of herself…of the situation…of him.

He needed to earn her trust. A woman who had been lied to and cheated on would look for honesty in a man. Faithfulness.

The relationship was new. At the moment, it was fueled by a palpable sexual chemistry. He didn't know where this was headed. But for now, he would give Layla what she needed. He would keep her safe.

Layla took a hot, super-quick shower. She had washed her hair that morning, so all she had to do was tuck it into the hotel-provided shower cap and use the extra time to shave her legs.

The bathroom door was locked. By her. Was that weird? Now, when she turned off the water, she listened carefully. If Joshua had returned already, he wasn't making a sound.

Staring at herself in the mirror was a mistake. She looked more scared than aroused. But that wasn't true. She wasn't scared of Josh.

Her body ached for his touch.

Maybe she was so comfortable being sexually vulnerable with him because their relationship hadn't begun recently. Admittedly, a years-long gap meant she didn't know him as well as she once had.

But she was convinced the essence of the man was the same.

She dried off and slipped into one of the silky nightgowns she had packed. Lots of women preferred black when they wanted to look sexy for a partner. Layla fared better in lighter, brighter colors. This sapphire blue set flattered her pale skin and blond hair.

Finally, she knew she couldn't dally any longer. She brushed her teeth. Put everything back in her toiletry kit. Took a deep breath. Showtime…

When she entered the bedroom from the bathroom, she thought for a moment that Josh still wasn't back. But then he moved, and she saw him. He had been standing at the window, half hidden by the heavy navy drapes.

A streak of dark red colored his cheekbones. "You look amazing," he said gruffly.

"Thanks." She didn't know what to do with her hands. Suddenly, she felt awkward, really awkward. "Your turn in the bathroom," she chirped brightly.

Josh closed the distance between them, took her in his arms and kissed her hungrily. "Don't be nervous, angel. That's what you look like. The angel on top of a Christmas tree. Perfect in every way."

She shook her head. "I'm not perfect, Josh. Nobody is." His embrace made her melt. All her reservations vanished. "I'm just a woman who wants to enjoy a sexy, interesting man. All night long."

"Hell, yeah," he muttered.

She pushed at his shoulders. "Go. I'll be waiting."

When he vanished into the bathroom, she folded back the covers on the bed and tested the sheets with her hand. Smooth as a baby's bottom. Cool and pristine.

She tossed aside most of the decorative pillows and chose two of the best ones to prop against the headboard. For the first time since meeting Josh again, a thought flitted through her mind. What if Josh was her forever guy, her chance to start over, to have a *real*, lasting relationship?

After her engagement to Richard ended, she had been more dispirited than heartbroken. She had known for some time that he wasn't the man she thought she knew. It showed up in little things. The way he was careless with her feelings. The many times he broke simple silly promises. Or forgot plans they made together.

With the hindsight of two long years, she had come to believe that she *made* herself think Richard was her heart's desire, because she was hitting that dreaded "thirty" mark, and she had wanted what so many of her friends had. Love. Stability.

In retrospect, Richard wasn't entirely to blame. The signs had been there, but Layla ignored them.

The cheating, though, that had broken her. It made her feel cheap and used, as if all Richard wanted was an in with her family, and once he accomplished that, he no longer had to pretend. Honestly, she stayed with him longer than she should have, because she was embarrassed to admit to her family how badly she had messed up.

It had been Chelsea who first saw the problems, Chelsea who encouraged Layla to dump a toxic relationship. For that, Layla would always be grateful to her older sister.

When the bathroom door swung open, Layla lost all interest in the past. The tall, lanky man—naked except for the fluffy hotel towel wrapped around his narrow hips—stood framed in the doorway with a charming grin.

Layla pretended to fan her face. "Oh my," she said. "I'm feeling a little woozy. All that testosterone…"

Josh chuckled. "That's the Layla I remember. Smart and sarcastic." He dropped a handful of packets on the table, crawled in bed beside her and nuzzled his face against her belly. "You smell delightful," he said, the words muffled.

She combed her finger through his thick, damp hair. "It's the hotel shower gel. You do, too."

Josh lifted his head and frowned. "I remember you always did have trouble taking a compliment. Even as a kid."

"I guess I thought you and Jordan only tolerated me. So if you said something nice, I didn't know how to take it."

He sat up. "And now?"

His gaze was serious. Her fingers itched to explore all that smooth, tanned skin. But he expected an answer.

"Well," she said slowly. "I think men tell women what they want to hear."

His expression darkened. "I'm neither a liar nor a cheat. And I was faithful to my wedding vows, for what it's worth."

"I know that, but…" She wrinkled her nose. "I was expecting more crazy sex with you, not a heart-to-heart."

He leaned on one elbow now, his head propped on his hand. She didn't like the way he seemed able to see inside her brain.

Josh's sculpted lips twisted in self-derision. "So you're not really interested in us getting to know each other better? You'd rather me bang you on the hood of a car and call it a day?" His mood was surly.

"Don't be crude. Of course not."

"Sure sounds like what you said."

"I'm not great with feelings." The words slipped out, involuntarily released from the truth vault. The Grandin family wasn't mushy.

His expression softened. "Come here, sexy thing."

She allowed him to tug her down and ease her onto her back. Now he leaned over her, surrounding her with his warmth and his delicious masculinity. "I thought guys liked to get straight to the main event," she muttered, feeling incredibly vulnerable amidst a warm, sultry arousal.

Josh toyed with one narrow strap of her nightgown. His fingers felt hot against her skin. The air-conditioning in the room worked very well. In fact, she *could* blame her tightly furled nipples on that very thing.

But again, she would be denying the truth. She ached to feel his hands on her bare body.

Her partner had more patience than she did. He traced her collarbone, then pulled both straps off her shoulders, trapping her upper arms. He kissed the sensitive skin below her ear. Nibbled her earlobe. Rubbed the curves of her breasts through thin silk.

"Josh…" She said his name raggedly. Pleading.

His smile was oddly sweet. "I'm glad my brother asked me to take his place on that date."

"Me, too," Layla said. "Very glad." She paused, wanting him to understand. "Everybody thinks I had a crush on Jordan when we were kids, and it's true, I did. But that's because he was easier than you. With Jordan, what you see is what you get."

"I'm not sure I understand." Josh's gaze was watchful, his expression wary.

"You're deeper. You have layers. That was true even back then. I was a little scared of you, I think, especially when we got to high school. You made me feel odd. I didn't know what to do with those emotions. They were the beginnings of sexual awareness. I realize that now. But for a girl of fifteen, those reactions were intimidating. It was simpler to field Jordan's dumb jokes than to talk to you."

"If I hadn't been a clueless adolescent boy, maybe I could have made it easier for both of us."

"Maybe." She ran her hand over the stubble on his chin, glad he hadn't felt the need to shave. "I sometimes envy those people who find their soul mate in high school. But broken engagements…broken marriages. They feel like failures, don't they?"

"Definitely. I guess most of us have to learn life's lessons the hard way."

She tugged his head down and kissed him, shivering when his tongue stroked hers possessively. When she could breathe, she rested her cheek against his chest. "I'm happy to continue this conversation later. But the gorgeous man in my bed needs attention."

Josh laughed. "*He* does, or you do?"

When she slipped her hand beneath the towel and wrapped her fingers around his erection, he groaned. It was Layla's turn to grin. "Both, I think."

Perhaps because things had moved so fast between them in the beginning, now they were able to momentarily harness the need, to bank the embers.

"I want to touch you all over," she complained. Her arms were still trapped at her sides.

Josh ignored her pleas. Slowly, ever so slowly, he dragged the bodice of her nightgown to her waist. As he tongued her nipples and bit them gently, Layla clenched her fingers in the sheet at her hips. The sensation was indescribable.

His voice, when he spoke, was low and raspy. "You were a cute kid…and an even cuter young teenager. But, Layla, you've grown into a stunning woman."

The raw sincerity in his words couldn't be feigned. The way he looked at her made Layla want to believe in fairy tales. The ones where the prince claimed his maiden.

Her body was on fire. "Get me out of this," she begged.

He finished removing her nightgown. Now she was naked. She tugged at his damp bath towel until she could pull it from under his hips and toss it on the floor.

Josh stared at her. "I want to devour you, and I'm not sure how I feel about that. You make me reckless. Desperate."

"It must be contagious." She ran her hands over his taut abdomen and up his broad chest to his pecs. Her fingernails dug into his shoulders. "Maybe foreplay is overrated. I need you now. I want you now."

The relief on his face told her they were on the same page. He grabbed protection, sheathed himself and moved between her legs. But he paused, the skin stretched tight over his cheekbones, his eyes glittering. "Maybe after the first fifty or sixty times, we'll want to slow down."

Layla wrapped her legs around his waist. "Don't bet on it, cowboy."

When he surged deep, she couldn't breathe for a moment. It wasn't his weight on top of her that was the problem. He had braced himself on his elbows.

The lack of oxygen was *forgetting* to breathe. As Josh buried himself inside her, bumping up against the deepest reaches of her sex, shock jumbled her synapses. All of her senses went on overload. She was hot and cold at the same time. Trembling with exhilaration and at the same moment teetering on the brink of despair.

Nothing this good could last. Nothing this good was real.

Were they both courting sexual oblivion to avoid their problems?

It felt as if she was flying without a net. Perilously close to crashing into oblivion.

His harsh breathing mingled with hers. The words he uttered were sexual and earthy. Praise and pleading. Her body raced to a climax that exploded in her pelvis and behind her eyelids in shards of blinding light.

She whimpered and lifted into his thrusts, desperate for every last ounce of completion.

When Josh cursed and went rigid, she knew he had found the same bliss.

They dozed afterward. She didn't know how long. When she tried to get up and go to the bathroom, Josh clasped her wrist. "Don't go," he said, slurring the words.

"I'll be right back." She kissed his hand and freed herself.

A few minutes later, she crawled back under the covers and burrowed into his embrace. His body was hot and hard and so wonderfully different from hers. She slipped one of her legs between his powerful thighs and stretched an arm across his chest.

For the first time in her life, she didn't question her future. It was enough to let things unfold one day at a time. She would live in the moment.

She yawned, replete and content, and let the waves of mental, physical and emotional exhaustion wash over her.

Nine

When Josh jerked awake in the middle of the night, he had no clue where he was. Gradually, his racing heart slowed. Had he been dreaming? A nightmare?

Then reason returned. And a grateful embrace of reality. Layla was in his arms. Soft, warm, deeply unconscious. She made the cutest little snuffling noises when she slept.

He cataloged his physical state. Sexually sated, but with a boner that could pound nails. Still unsure about the future except to know that at this very moment an anonymous hotel room with this very specific woman was exactly where he wanted to be.

They had fallen asleep early. Now he'd had

enough rest to be energized already. But it would be selfish to wake Layla.

Surreptitiously, he peered at his watch. One thirty in the morning. His stomach was growling, and he needed to visit the john. Carefully, he moved a feminine arm. Then a leg. Layla grumbled in her sleep, turned away from him, but didn't wake up.

While he took care of business and washed up, all he thought about was making love to her again. He was rusty about dating rules. Could a guy get in trouble for coaxing a drowsy woman into having sex?

When he rejoined her, she recoiled from his cold feet. He moved them, but drew her closer, spooning her and filling his hands with her breasts. The curves and valleys were delightful. He could almost be satisfied with this.

But his body urged him to take more.

He wanted more. In fact, he trembled with the need to be inside her.

"Layla." He whispered her name, willing her to wake up. "Layla, sweetheart. Can you open your eyes?"

It seemed like eons, but it was probably only a minute or two.

She rolled onto her back and shoved the hair out of her eyes. "What?"

That single grumpy syllable didn't bode well for his plans. "I was hoping you might want to…you know…" He stroked her center.

Layla made a noise that was halfway between a protest and a moan.

"Was that a *yes*?" he asked hopefully.

"Do you have something against sleep?" Her sarcastic question was clearly rhetorical.

He kissed her, sliding his tongue deep into her mouth. Then he nuzzled her nose with his. "How can I sleep when a gorgeous, naked woman is in my bed driving me insane with her incredible body?"

"Over the top, Banks. Over the top."

He rubbed his erection against her thigh. "I'm dead serious. So serious."

Because there was a light burning in the bathroom, and he had left the door cracked, he could see the grin that finally lifted the corners of her mouth, even though her eyes remained stubbornly closed. "Single-minded, aren't you?"

He played with her breasts one at a time, teasing the nipples. Plumping the curves. "I'm gonna need a clear affirmative from you, Ms. Grandin. Audible consent. Please."

Finally, her long lashes lifted. Her blue eyes looked darker in the dim light. "Yes, Mr. Banks. I agree to have sex with you. Under one condition."

He tensed. "What is it?"

"You've got to feed me afterward. I'm starving."

Twenty minutes later, Josh flopped onto his back, his chest heaving. "Damn, woman. What was that thing you did with your tongue?"

Layla giggled, a young, innocent sound that was more like the girl he had once known than the sophisticated, capable woman with whom he had recently reconnected.

She yawned and stretched. "If we're going to have sex this much, I may need to bring snacks and a cooler."

"Okay, okay," he said rolling out of bed to fetch the room service menu. "What do you want?"

With a naked Josh sitting four feet away in all his glory, Layla *knew* what she wanted. But at this point in the relationship, it seemed prudent not to give the man any more ammunition than necessary. "Nachos?" she said.

He winced. "Seriously?"

"Fine," she huffed. "You throw out a suggestion."

"No. I'll give you one more chance."

"We could split a burger."

His gaze narrowed. "Medium rare?"

"Is there any other way?"

"Cheese?" he asked.

"Swiss and cheddar both."

"I can see you like to live on the edge."

She stretched her arms over her head, enjoying the way his gaze settled on her breasts and glazed over. "You would know. And it's all your fault. I was practically a nun before you came back to town. I think you've corrupted me."

Josh tossed the menu aside and ran a hand up the inside of her thigh, his eyes flashing fire, his cheeks flushing. "Room service can wait," he groaned. When he buried his face between her legs, she shrieked.

It was three o'clock before they got any food.

Layla sighed. "That might be the best cheese-burger I've ever eaten."

They were tucked up in bed, shoulder to shoulder, devouring their meal. Layla had insisted on protecting the fancy comforter with a couple of bath towels.

Josh leaned toward her and licked her chin. "Ketchup," he explained solemnly.

She batted his hand away when he tried to tug at the sheet she used to protect her modesty. "Behave."

He shrugged. "If you insist." After snitching a handful of fries from her plate because his were all gone, he shot her a sideways glance. "I want to know more about the grown-up Layla. What is it you love about the ranch?"

She smiled. "That's easy. The horses. I tell them all my secrets. I love the way they move and the joy they feel when they gallop. The smell of hay in the barns. The way the mares whinny when they want the colts to settle for the night."

Josh was silent for so long, she felt self-conscious.

"What?" she demanded. "Was that more than you wanted to know?"

"That was beautiful," he said gruffly.

She ate another french fry, because it was something to do. "Not everything at the ranch is so po-etic. I'm handy with the business part. I've got an

MBA that I put to good use when Grandy and Dad let me." She stopped, overwhelmed anew by the remembrance that her grandfather was gone.

Josh slid an arm around her shoulders, comforting her without words. He sighed. "They're lucky to have you."

"I don't know," she said honestly, ruefully. "I've been thinking it might be time for me to move on."

"Why?"

"Well, if Daddy goes by Grandy's example, he'll clutch the reins until he's old and gray. And even then, Vic will be the one to take over. I'm not sure there's any point in me staying in the long term. I've thought about finding something else to do with my life. Maybe after my grandmother is gone. I don't want to disappoint her."

"I can't imagine you being a disappointment to anyone."

"That's sweet," she said. But Josh didn't see the whole picture. Layla had disappointed her parents right out of the gate by not being a boy. Chelsea was bad enough. But now *two* girls? Only the advent of Vic had satisfied the familial expectations. And poor Morgan was likely supposed to be a boy, too, to even the scales.

Layla set her plate on the bedside table. "I should probably get some more sleep," she said. "I need to be at the hospital by nine."

"Of course."

They put the room service tray out in the hall and

locked the door. Josh turned out the light. It was silent for a moment as they got comfortable under the covers. He didn't allow any distance between them.

Layla's eyes were closed when he spoke.

"You can stay here as long as you want, if you can be away from the ranch."

She studied his words for hidden meanings. Was he simply being nice, or was that an ongoing booty call? "Thank you," she said. "I suppose it will depend on Grammy. When they release her, I'll need to be out there to help."

"Makes sense."

She rested her cheek on his shoulder. "Why are you staying in this hotel instead of with your dad and brother?"

Something in him reacted. He either flinched or froze or *something*. At last, he answered her. "My brother asked me the same thing. I've been gone for a long time. I've needed space to do some thinking about what comes next."

"I thought you wanted to come home."

"I did. I do. But sometimes life takes a turn we don't expect."

Layla pretended to fall asleep after that. What did he mean?

Soon, she heard him breathing deeply. He was out cold.

Unfortunately, Layla was awake far longer, wondering if she was making a huge mistake. She liked Josh a lot. They had a history of sorts. He was the kind of man she could fall in love with…could marry. Start a family with.

Was she weaving crazy dreams?

Maybe *she* needed some space, too. Her world had been turned upside down in the last month. She was emotionally vulnerable. Perhaps it was time to take a step back and protect herself.

Josh ordered breakfast from room service while Layla was in the shower. The sun was bright, too bright for his eyes, which were gritty from lack of sleep. But he wouldn't change a thing.

When Layla exited the bathroom, she was fully dressed. And in a hurry.

She grimaced when she saw the food. "I'm so sorry, Josh. I don't have time to linger. I'm trying to get to the hospital before the doctor comes by." She kissed his cheek on the way to the door. "I'll let you know how Grammy is doing. Bye."

The door closed with a gentle slam. And then Josh was alone.

He ate two thirds of the food and left the rest. When he was dressed and ready, he pulled out his phone and checked flight schedules. If he hurried, he could catch a midmorning hop to Dallas and be back before bedtime. He had a few loose ends to tie up.

It was a long day. Air travel was becoming more and more of an endurance test. He could have chartered a small jet. But it seemed like an unnecessary expense at this juncture. So he endured the packed plane and the inevitable delays.

By the time he made it back to Royal, retrieved his car and drove from the airport to the hotel, he was exhausted. Only the prospect of seeing Layla again kept him going.

It was an unpleasant shock to enter his room and find no sign of the woman who had kept him awake half the night.

Only a note on the pillow gave him a clue.

He read it with a sinking feeling.

"Hey, Josh—Grammy was doing so well the doctor released her right after dinner this evening. We've all headed back to the ranch. I stopped by to grab my suitcase as I'm sure you've noticed. Thanks again for rescuing me on the street and for such a fun night. Talk soon, Layla."

He crumpled the sheet Layla had torn from a hotel notepad. Tossing it in the nearest wastebasket gave him a moment's satisfaction. But then he reneged and rescued it, flattening the paper between his fingers.

The depth of his disappointment was significant. Instead of another night of hot, wonderful sex, he was going to sleep alone.

Without Layla.

How had she come to be so important to him so quickly?

He slept fitfully and awoke at dawn. Though he had put it off, he knew it was time for a serious talk with his father and brother.

Three cups of coffee later, he was headed out to the Bankses' ranch. Their property was prosperous and productive, but not on the scale of either the Grandins' or the Lattimores'. Those two families were Royal royalty. He grinned at his own joke.

When he came here recently, the three men had spent most of their time in the barn and on horses riding the property. Today, as Josh walked into the warm, cozy kitchen at the old farmhouse, it was almost as if nothing at all had changed in the last week or the last decade. His dad and his twin brother were seated at the scarred oak table eating pancakes.

Jordan looked up with a grin. "We saved you some," he said. "Pull up a chair."

While Josh ate, his father read the *New York Times*. Jordan stared at his phone.

They had never been the kind of family to wade into deep conversational waters. Which made what Josh was about to do all the more difficult.

Eventually, he finished his meal and screwed up his courage. "Hey, you two. I have a question to ask. And I need you to think about it before you answer."

Each man looked up with an identical expression of bewilderment.

Bertram waved a hand. "Well, don't keep us in suspense."

Josh swallowed hard. "Would the two of you consider buying out my share of the ranch?"

Jordan's mouth fell open.

Josh's dad paled. "Hell, son. We were just razzing you the other day…giving you a hard time. Of course we want you back. You have to know that."

Josh's brother nodded. "We're excited to have you home."

"I believe you—I do. But I'm not sure staying is the right choice for me. Clearly, I don't have a great track record with big life changes. Still, it seems to me that the two of you have things running smoothly here. I know I could help, but it would be the path of least resistance. I really want to try something new."

Bertram stood and refilled his coffee cup. "Like what?" His father had been perturbed to hear Josh had quit his job.

"I'm not sure. I don't have everything pinned down yet. But as soon as I land on a plan, you'll be the first to know, I swear."

Jordan shook his head slowly. "Cash flow is not a problem. We're doing better than we ever have. If you want us to buy you out, Dad and I can swing it. But you wouldn't be a third wheel here at the ranch. You're family. You're my brother, my twin."

Josh was taken aback when Jordan hugged him spontaneously. He returned the hug, realizing how much he had given up when he moved away. "Thanks," he said, his throat tight. "That means a lot. You know I love this ranch. It's home. But you two have made it what it is. I think I need to let this be your baby. I'm going to carve out something for myself—or I will if I'm lucky. Call it an early midlife crisis, I guess. The divorce rattled me. I don't want to screw up my life that badly ever again."

Layla hadn't seen Josh in ten days. It seemed impossible, but the hours flew by. Taking care of Grammy kept the family busy. Her medications had been worked out, of course, but she seemed frail after her collapse. Too much stress, perhaps.

The family had fallen into a schedule that was working for the moment. Chelsea, Layla and Morgan split up the waking hours. Layla's parents and brother took turns occupying the extra twin bed in Grammy's bedroom overnight. It was the one Victor Senior had slept in.

Miriam was grieving. They all were. But each day got a little easier.

One afternoon when Layla was off the clock, she went for a drive, needing to get out of the house and clear her head. Caring for her grandmother had turned out to be the perfect distraction to avoid thinking about Josh.

What was she going to do about him?

The two of them hadn't even talked on the phone. But they had texted now and then. She presumed he was busy, though he didn't give her any details, and she didn't ask. Miriam's health was the usual topic of conversation.

One night late, Layla got a short text.

I miss you…

Her heart did a funny little flip in her chest. She felt like a teenage girl crushing on a boy who smiled at her.

I miss you, too...

That was it. Just those two texts. And then nothing. But she wondered if Josh was just missing the sex, or did he really have feelings for her?

It was hard to read his mind. Not that she had been particularly forthcoming about her own feelings. Thinking about Josh made her ache. Though she had tried to downplay her emotions, even to herself, the truth was impossible to ignore. She was maybe/possibly falling for Joshua Banks.

He was likely being a gentleman, trying to respect the fact that Layla had a lot of responsibilities at the moment.

She drove aimlessly at first, leaving the town limits and seeking out the open road. Sunshine and blue skies were mood boosters, but it wasn't enough.

Eventually, she found herself headed toward the spot where Josh had made love to her for the first time. When she found the small hilltop, she parked her car and got out. If she closed her eyes, she could remember that afternoon in Technicolor detail.

There had been so much urgency, so much heat. The attraction wasn't one-sided. That much she knew. They had both been hungry, desperate to connect in the most intimate ways possible.

Thinking of those hours made her face hot with a blush that emanated from deep inside her. *Wanton* and *reckless* were not words she associated with herself.

But with Josh, she felt like a different person.

When she spent the night with him at the hotel, the magnetic lure had only strengthened. Pheromones on steroids.

Could that kind of sexual compatibility be only physical? Sex with Richard had been enjoyable. But not earth-shattering. Why were she and Josh combustible?

She didn't want to believe she had deep feelings for him. He was coming off a messy divorce. Admittedly, he and his wife hadn't been together in over two years before that. But still. The man might have a few *issues*.

Most friends she knew who had divorced weren't eager to jump back into any kind of serious relationship.

The Spring Luncheon at the Cattleman's Club was coming up very soon. Josh had agreed to be her date. Would that be the end of this fling or the beginning of a new chapter?

Truthfully, she was scared to make the next move. Josh had the power to hurt her, though he might not realize it. If he wasn't interested in anything more than sex, she would have to extricate herself gracefully.

She knew people who enjoyed physical affairs

without messy entanglements, but Layla wasn't made that way.

As the wind cooled her skin and sent her hair flying around her head, she knew this was a critical point in her life. She had never found validation in her family. Not really. To them, she was just Layla. Always around. Always available.

But surely there was more to life than being the middle child of four, as odd as that sounded. Who was she? What did she want? Was she willing to fight for Josh? Really, it was more than that. She could bring peace and purpose and challenge to her life with or without a man. Suddenly, one of the puzzle pieces fell into place.

Excitement buzzed in her veins. She spared one last wistful glance for the place where she had first felt the warmth of Josh's single-minded lovemaking, and then she drove quickly back into town.

One of her college classmates was a Realtor now. Layla burst into her office, out of breath and hopeful. Shana was a successful Black woman who possessed the kind of personality that made her a natural with customers.

After they exchanged pleasantries, Layla handed over her phone, where she had captured a screenshot of latitude and longitude. "I want to find out about this property," she said. "It looks like an old farm that hasn't been worked in years. I might want to buy it if the price is right."

Shana stared at the photo and then typed something into her computer. And then more. She frowned. "The owners were elderly. They died back in January, both of them. They had two heirs, a son and a daughter in their sixties. The property was definitely for sale, but now the listing says *not available*."

Layla's heart sank. "What does that mean? It doesn't say *sold*?"

"I'll get to the bottom of it," Shana promised. "And in the meantime, why don't I start looking for other properties? You can email me a list of what features you're interested in…acreage…etc. I know I can find something you'll like."

"Thanks," Layla said. "I appreciate it."

Ten

Back in the car, Layla blew her nose, trying to swallow the disappointment that made her eyes sting. She'd been on an impulsive errand anyway. In her head, she had already been building a cute house, right on the spot where Josh parked his car with a view of the surrounding countryside.

How silly and sad was that? Memorializing one amazing encounter with a man who was as mysterious as he was sexy.

Back at home, she found Chelsea on the back porch having coffee. "Where have *you* been?" her older sister asked.

"I went for a drive."

"To see Josh Banks?" Chelsea asked it with a teasing smile. Layla had shared only the G-rated details of her time with Josh.

"Nope. I don't think he's interested in anything serious. And besides, I've had far too much humiliation to go chasing after another man who doesn't know what the word *commitment* means."

"I can't imagine Joshua Banks cheating on a woman. He's always been a straight arrow, hasn't he?"

"He has. But I think that proves my point. It's been over a week. He hasn't asked me out again. I imagine he has other things on his mind besides me."

"I'm sorry, Layla. I could hear in your voice how much you liked him."

"It's not just that. I'm thinking about leaving the ranch. Dad is hung up on this Vic idea, and even if he ever relents, *you'll* be the logical choice to run things, not me. I've been the invisible Grandin my whole life. Is it selfish of me to want a guy to think I hung the moon? To give me his undying devotion?"

That last part was tongue-in-cheek. Chelsea heard the underlying plea and hugged her tightly. "You have to know that you're always welcome here, no matter who's in charge. And as for wanting more in the relationship department, well, don't give up on men."

"I'm not. But they sure make life complicated." She was ready to shift the subject to something less personal. "By the way, I forgot to tell you about one unpleasant experience I had."

"With Josh?" Chelsea seemed shocked.

"Not exactly. He and I were having dinner when this strange man showed up at our table. He introduced himself as Nolan Thurston, *Heath* Thurston's brother."

Now Chelsea's face reflected even more shock. "What did he do? What did he want? Did he threaten you?"

"Oh, no. Exactly the opposite. He asked if you and I might have lunch with him to *talk things out*. He thought we could come to some kind of understanding, I guess. But you know he was probably a spy for his brother…trying to find out what our family knows about the oil rights situation…what we're thinking."

"He hasn't contacted you again?" Chelsea asked.

"No. That's why I forgot about it until now. Why on earth do you care?"

"Well, it might not hurt for us to do the same. Get information from him. Strengthen our position."

"I don't want to have anything to do with either of the Thurstons." Layla still felt guilty about keeping her grandmother's secret.

"Oh, well. It may be a nonissue." Chelsea stood and collected her cup and saucer. "Will you sit with Grandmother for half an hour? I'm supposed to relieve Morgan, but I've got an important Zoom call. Won't take me long."

"Sure," Layla said.

When she reached Grammy's room, Morgan put

a finger to her lips. "Shh," she whispered. "She just fell asleep."

The two women stepped out into the hall. "How is she?" Layla asked.

Morgan smiled. "Really good overall. She's eating well. But I know she's grieving more than she wants us to see. You hear about people in long marriages dying of broken hearts when they lose a partner. It's selfish, I guess, but I hope she won't go too soon. I need Grammy. We all do."

"Definitely." Layla surveyed her baby sister's red hair and blue eyes and the shadows under those eyes. Morgan was the only one in the family who didn't work on the ranch. She owned a boutique in town called The Rancher's Daughter. It surely hadn't been easy to find the time to help out, but she had carried her share of the load.

Layla spoke impulsively. "Why don't you let me cover your hours tomorrow? You look beat."

Morgan's expression was wistful. "I'm tired, yes. And I appreciate the offer. But I feel so conscious now that our time with her is limited. I don't want to have any regrets."

"I understand. Still, if the shop and all this gets to be too much, let me know."

When Layla slipped quietly into the dimly lit bedroom, her grandmother opened her eyes, her expression mutinous. "I could hear the two of you whispering out in the hall. Talking about me, I'll bet. I'm not an invalid."

Layla sat down beside the bed. "Of course you're not. We were just being quiet because Morgan said you were asleep. Were you playing possum?"

That made Grammy smile. "I *was* asleep," she said. "But it was just a catnap." She sat up in the bed. "Will you take me to the back porch? I need some sun."

"Sure. It's a beautiful day."

Miriam Grandin wasn't about to accept help she didn't need. Though Layla held the wheelchair steady, her grandmother stood up and then seated herself. Layla tucked a fluffy afghan around her knees. "Here we go."

The old woman perked up even more when they got outside. When the housekeeper checked on them, Layla asked for cookies and cocoa. The calendar might say spring, but it was never out of season for Grammy's favorites.

With the wheelchair by the porch rail, Miriam could tip her face toward the sky. "This is nice," she said. "I'm damn tired of staying inside."

Layla smothered a snort of laughter. She loved her grandmother's indomitable spirit. Morgan probably didn't have a thing to worry about.

"Well," she said. "You're doing great. I don't see why you can't gradually get back to your normal schedule."

"The new normal, you mean."

The gentle rebuke reminded Layla that Victor

Grandin Sr. still cast a long shadow. "Yes, ma'am," she said meekly.

"So tell me what's going on with you and the Banks boy."

Layla flushed. "This family gossips more than the old biddies in town."

"You can't blame us. After the debacle with your Richard person, we just want to see you happy again."

"I'm happy," Layla muttered.

"Doesn't look like it at the moment. You should be out having fun. Now that I'm not at death's door anymore, I'll hire a nice girl to sit with me during the day. The rest of you need to get on with your lives."

"We love you, Grammy."

"I know that. But you've done enough."

Layla wouldn't win that argument, so she changed the subject. Her grandmother was strong enough now to have this discussion. "Grammy," she said. "Don't you think we need to tell the others about Grandy's journal? I feel bad keeping it from them."

Miriam shrugged. "No point in it. Without the paperwork, that journal doesn't mean a thing. It wouldn't hold up in court. Relax, girl. That fancy-ass investigator my son hired will follow the trail. Time enough to worry about things when his work is done."

"Okay..." Layla didn't want to go against her grandmother's wishes. And in this case, maybe she was right. The legalities were what mattered. No substantiated paperwork, no claim.

Three days later, Layla stood in front of the full-length mirror in her closet and surveyed her choice of outfit. Josh was picking her up for the noon event at the Texas Cattleman's Club in an hour. She had already changed three times.

First, she had picked out a tangerine Jackie O–style dress. It was sophisticated and springlike, but she didn't feel quite right in it. Next there was a trendy pantsuit, teal with a floral silk blouse to match. The cut of the jacket and pants flattered her figure, but again, she gave it a thumbs-down.

Now she wore a riskier choice. The dress she had chosen was blush-pink silk with a low neckline and spaghetti straps. The waist was fitted, then flared into a flirty skirt that stopped a few inches above her knees.

The layered skirt alternated between the lighter pink silk and a more vivid rosy shade of tulle that peeked out when she moved. Her shoes were three-inch heels in a nude color that didn't detract from the dress.

Jewelry had been a hard choice, but she settled on a single-diamond pendant that rode demurely on the slope of her breasts. Matching studs adorned her ears.

Last, but not least, she carried a pink-flamingo

clutch that perfectly completed the underlayers of her skirt.

On a normal day at the club, this outfit would definitely be over-the-top. But the Spring Luncheon was a notable social event. Layla wouldn't stand out for being overdressed. Though the men would be in dark suits, the female plumage would run the gamut.

Last year, one of Layla's old high school classmates—renowned for making an entrance wherever she went—showed up in skintight silver lamé. The gossipmongers had a field day with that one. But not long after, the woman snagged husband number two, so as a strategy, it worked.

Layla's heart raced, and her cheeks matched her dress. The wardrobe choice wasn't the only thing giving her heartburn. It was the text she'd received earlier from Josh.

I'd like for you to spend the rest of the afternoon and evening with me. If you're interested, pack a bag...

On the one hand, she loved his direct communication. It was clear and to the point. But why had he waited so long to coax her into his bed again? To be fair, she had disappeared from his hotel room after the first time and only left a note. But surely he understood why.

Though she had a ton of reservations about getting in deeper with a sexual relationship that might never progress to anything else, she didn't have the will to say no.

She wanted Josh. It was risky. It made her vulnerable.

But she couldn't give up a man who made her feel both exhilarated and safe. It was a fascinating combination.

Though it seemed silly, she didn't put her suitcase on the bed. She kept it in the closet and packed it surreptitiously, not wanting Chelsea to wander in and ask uncomfortable questions.

A family friend was coming to sit with Grammy. No one had been hired yet. Only Grammy thought that was a good idea.

The remaining six Grandins were going together to the club. Except for Layla. She had invented an excuse about having to leave earlier. No one had questioned her. If she was lucky, she could go down the stairs that exited the side of the house. She had asked Josh not to ring the bell, but to text her when he arrived.

If he thought the request odd, he didn't let on.

Her phone dinged at exactly 11:13. Her ride was two minutes early. It wasn't a forty-five-minute drive to the club, but Layla wanted to disappear from the house before her parents and siblings congregated.

She tucked her purse under her arm, checked her reflection one last time and picked up the small suitcase. It wasn't heavy. A woman didn't need much when she was planning on being naked most of the time.

She choked back a laugh as she tiptoed down the stairs. When she rounded the corner of the house, Josh was standing beside his car. From the look on his face, she had to assume her outfit was on point.

He shook his head slowly as he looked her over from head to toe, his eyes flashing with male appreciation. "You look incredible, Layla. Are you sure we have to go to the Cattleman's Club luncheon?"

The question was clearly rhetorical. She hoped. "Thank you for the compliment, but I need to see and be seen," she said, smiling. "We're fighting this oil rights claim, so all the Grandins will be front and center today."

He reached out and took her suitcase. After placing it in the trunk of his car, he came around and opened the passenger side. "In you go." He tucked pieces of her flyaway skirt beneath her leg before carefully closing the door.

When he was behind the wheel with the engine started and the AC blowing cool air, he faced her. His expression was not so lighthearted now.

"What's wrong?" she asked, experiencing a fillip of alarm.

"I've missed you," he said gruffly. Carefully, he leaned forward and kissed her cheek. Then he followed it up with a second one just below her ear.

Everything inside her went on high alert. Wow. With only two chaste kisses, the man could make the cells in her body sizzle with wanting him.

When she would have pressed closer, he held her

at arm's length with a rueful smile. His hands were warm on her bare shoulders. "No more," he said. "If I start kissing you like I really want to, we'll never get to the club."

For half a second, she debated blowing off the big event and going back to Josh's hotel room. Unfortunately, she had always been the conscientious type.

Sometimes being a mature, responsible adult sucked.

Josh gripped the steering wheel with damp hands. His throat was dry. His chest was tight. Layla was everything he wanted in a woman. Smart. Funny. Sexy as hell. The faint scent of her perfume made the confines of the car a torture chamber for a man desperate to get laid ASAP. Seeing Layla appear with suitcase in hand moments ago had been a huge relief.

He hadn't been one hundred percent positive she wanted a do-over.

She looked different today, and it wasn't just the clothes, though that dress was tantalizing and provocative. Her body was curved in all the right places.

Maybe it was the way she wore her hair. This morning, it was twisted on top of her head in the kind of intricate style women seem to instinctively know how to do.

Unfortunately, the updo bared the provocative feminine real estate at the top of her spine. Which made Josh's hungry fascination about a thousand times more intense. All he could think about was nibbling the back of her neck while he reached around and cupped her bare breasts.

And they *would* be bare. No matter how gorgeous the dress, he planned to have her out of it as soon as possible.

Already, he was calculating how long they would have to stay at the club before he could spirit her away.

"You're awfully quiet today," he said as he threaded his way through the streets of Royal proper.

Layla sighed. "I've been looking forward to seeing you again, but I'm worried about the two of us."

"Why is that?"

"I'm in my thirties already. I should have my life together by now. But I've held men at a distance, because I felt so betrayed and rejected by Richard. I wish I could say I was in love with him, but I wasn't. And you've admitted you weren't in love with your wife. Not the kind of forever love we're supposed to want."

"Where are you going with this, Layla? No offense, but we're pulling up at the club in about six and a half minutes. Not exactly the time for a heart-to-heart."

"That's probably why I did it," she said. "I'm scared to get hurt again." She half turned in her seat. Now he sensed her staring at him, even though he kept his eyes on the road. "You're a great guy," she said. "But…"

"But what?" He felt his blood pressure rise, and not in a pleasant way.

Layla twisted a piece of her skirt restlessly. "Statistics for divorced people aren't good when it comes to future success with new partners."

"You sound like you've been reading encyclopedias," he grumbled, feeling his neck get hot. He *was* divorced. No way around it. If he could go back and undo all his mistakes, he would. But he was stuck with his checkered past. The missteps had taught him what was valuable and what was dross.

"I don't think encyclopedias exist anymore, do they?" she said.

"We're getting off track." He pulled into a parking space, slammed the car into Park and faced her, trying not to glower. "If you and I together is such a risky proposition, why did you bring a suitcase?"

Layla's bottom lip trembled. Her dewy cheeks were flushed—a shade of pink that almost matched her dress. Her blue eyes shimmered with something he couldn't quite decipher. It almost looked as if she might cry, but that made no sense.

They were together. On a day that was supposed to be fun.

"You didn't answer my question," he said quietly. "Why did you bring a suitcase if you're breaking things off?"

Her chin came up. "I never said that. Besides, there's nothing to break off. You and I are friends."

"With benefits." He wouldn't let her brush aside the incredible moments when they had been intimate—

first at the picnic and later in his hotel room. "I assumed you didn't have sex with me on a whim."

"I didn't," she whispered.

"But you've changed your mind? Because you think I'm on the rebound, and you've got sucky taste in men? Is that it in a nutshell?"

"You should have been a lawyer, Josh." Her eyes shot blue sparks. "And for the record, I don't like being interrogated."

Years ago, he had learned to keep his temper under control. Now it popped and sizzled, dangerously close to igniting. "Then what *do* you like, Layla? Tell me."

Even though they were early, he had deliberately chosen a parking space at the far reaches of the parking lot. It meant they would have to walk a fair distance to get to the club entrance, but for now, there were no cars anywhere close to them. Which was a good thing, because this argument didn't need witnesses.

Her continued silence pushed him closer to the edge. "What *do* you like, Layla? If we're such an unlikely pair, what *do* you like?"

Without warning, she put both hands on the sides of his neck and pulled him closer. Now he could see the layers of blue in her pupils, layers that threatened to submerge him and drown him.

"I thought it was obvious," she said, the words husky. "I like having sex with you."

When Layla pressed her mouth to his, he jerked,

shocked and stunned and crazy in lust with her. "Yes," he stuttered as her tongue and lips dueled with his.

He slid a hand inside the top of her dress and found bare skin beneath what appeared to be a lacy nothing of a bra. He squeezed reverently. "I've laid awake every night thinking about this. About you."

She groaned, wrapping her arms around his neck and teasing the whorl of his ear with her talented tongue. "Yes."

What was she saying yes to? Was she having the same sleepless nights?

He rubbed her nipple, feeling it peak beneath his fingertips. "It scares me how much I want you," he confessed. It was true. Layla brought him peace and agitation in equal measure. Her presence in his arms helped him reclaim the contentment of his childhood when his biggest problem was how to keep his brother from eating the last ice-cream sandwich in the freezer. But touching her, making love to her, created the frenzied agitation of knowing he had no control when it came to Layla.

He was moments away from dragging her into the back seat and taking her wildly when some tiny voice inside his head whispered reason. Already, cars were lining up closer and closer in the parking lot. Today was a big deal, especially so for Layla and her family.

It took every ounce of determination he could muster to peel her arms from around his neck and ease her over into her seat. "Fix your lipstick," he muttered, already missing her warmth.

Her gaze was hazy and unfocused. There was a tiny red patch on her collarbone where he had nibbled her like the rarest of gourmet delights. She put a hand to her mouth. "What time is it?"

"A quarter till twelve."

"Oh my gosh." Frantically, she searched for her purse. The flamingo nested in the floor of the car. Layla grabbed it and found what she needed.

He pulled the visor down for her. "Don't worry. We didn't mess up much."

Not for the world would he mention that she had the look of a woman who had just experienced orgasmic pleasure. The dreamy expression in her eyes. Warm, glowing skin all over that made her seem young and lush. Lips puffy from his hungry kisses.

She was no ingenue, and yet she projected innocence and sweetness. The fact that she seemed unaware of her appeal made her all the sexier. When Layla was satisfied with her face and her hair, he shut off the engine. It was going to be a scorcher today.

He touched her arm. "Shall we make an appearance, Ms. Grandin?"

He saw Layla take a deep breath as she checked her reflection one last time. Then she curled her hand around his. "Thank you for bringing me today."

"Of course. And by the way, am I supposed to play the part of your adoring boyfriend, so the whole town will know Richard the ass is a distant memory?"

Her lips tilted up in a smile. "I like the way you think."

"The role isn't much of a stretch," he said, brushing the backs of his fingers across her soft cheek.

Big blue eyes searched his. Was she looking for assurance? The best way he could give her that was to keep showing up.

"Come on," he said. "Let's do this…"

Eleven

Layla had been coming to the Texas Cattleman's Club since she was a child. Sometimes her family enjoyed Sunday brunch on the terrace. On other occasions, she tagged along when her mother met friends for lunch. And then there were the holiday memories. The huge tree in the lobby entrance. The lavish parties. Cookies and stockings and other goodies. Adult laughter and conversation. Usually an appearance by Santa Claus.

As the daughter of a wealthy rancher, she had always been welcomed at the club. But even as a teenager, she had been aware of a rigid hierarchy that took some in and kept others out. Fortunately, in recent years as some of the old guard passed on and newer, more progressive ideas were incorporated, the membership had become more inclusive. Now she paid her dues like all the other members.

Josh had her arm tucked in his elbow. She liked how that felt. Honestly, she enjoyed the way other women in the room looked him over with interest. Though he'd told her he still maintained his TCC membership, it had probably been at least six or eight years since he had entered this historic building.

Appetizers were being served on small tables scattered around the main hallway. Fresh flowers hung from brass sconces. Someone had even whimsically decorated a stuffed moose head with a tiara of daisies.

Layla wasn't a particular fan of hunting trophies, but some of them remained, even after renovations and redecorating. A small brass plaque below each specimen recorded the hunter and the date. Taxidermists in Royal would always have a job.

She and Josh grabbed a couple of plates. The shrimp and cocktail sauce were legendary. Not to mention the tiny Angus beef sliders. "Pace yourself," she warned her companion. "You'll want to save room for lunch." She wiped her lips with a napkin. "Would you mind if I touch base with a few folks?"

He grinned. "With or without me?"

"Don't you know people?" she asked, cocking her head and staring at him to see if he was kidding.

"Go," he said. "It's been a while, but I still recognize half the folks in this room. I'll be fine."

She squeezed his hand and walked away, conscious of his gaze on her back. That little interlude in the car had left her with quivery knees and a marked lack of enthusiasm for socializing. Even so, she had work to do.

She found the Lattimores standing in two tight circles and greeted them a few at a time. Jonathan and Jayden. Alexa and Caitlyn. Their parents, Ben and Barbara.

Even though Alexa had flown in to attend the funeral of Layla's grandfather, she had returned for this event, probably at her parents' urging. Layla tugged her to a quiet corner. "How are things at your house?" she asked.

Alexa grimaced. Her long black curls and dark brown eyes made her stand out. The gorgeous Black woman sighed. "Like your family, everyone is worried about the oil rights business. And absolutely no one can understand why my grandfather would put *our* ranch at risk, when it was your uncle who fathered a child."

"I know I said it once, but you should really come home and help them. They need a lawyer they can trust. Surely your firm will give you a leave of absence… right? For a family crisis?"

"Poor naive Layla." Alexa grinned so Layla would know she was kidding. "My bosses are all about billable hours."

"But you'll try?"

"I don't know," Alexa said, looking torn. "It's not a good time for me."

"Emergencies never are."

Chelsea appeared at Layla's elbow, seeming out of breath. "Hey, Alexa," she said. "Glad to see you again. If you don't mind, I need to borrow my sister for a moment."

Alexa waved a hand. "She's all yours."

Before Layla could blink, Chelsea had backed her into a corner. Literally. Her older sister frowned. "I just peeked in the dining room. Your place card isn't at our table. Are you planning to skip the meal? Geez, Layla. You know this is an important day."

Layla shook her head slowly. "Calm down. Of course I know. Show of strength and all that."

"So why aren't you going to eat lunch?"

"Did it ever occur to you that my place card might be at another table?"

Chelsea's jaw dropped. "You're with someone?"

"Joshua Banks."

Chelsea's expression of bewilderment was comical. "But I thought you said that situation wasn't going anywhere. You told me you wanted someone with no emotional baggage, a man who would worship the ground you walk on."

"Now, you're editorializing." Layla laughed. "Relax. I'll be in the dining room the whole time. But Josh and I have a table for two."

"And *after* lunch?" Chelsea raised an eyebrow.

Layla felt her face get hot. "After lunch, we'll

see." She took her sister's arm. "Come on. Let's mingle for a few minutes. We need the support of the town if this oil rights business gets ugly. Schmoozing 'R' Us."

She and Chelsea worked the room for fifteen minutes. Then the president of the club announced that lunch was ready to be served. En masse, the crowd of people began moving toward the dining room.

Chelsea went up on her tiptoes. "So where *is* Joshua Banks? Surely you didn't leave him alone in this room of female piranhas."

Layla might have miscalculated. Josh was fresh meat on the social scene. Why hadn't she thought of that? "He'll be fine," she said, hoping her words were true.

Suddenly, she spotted him, and her vision narrowed. *Wow.* Chelsea saw him at the same moment. She whistled under her breath. "Your man looks pretty darned gorgeous in that tailored suit. The Joshua I remember didn't have a body like that. He was skinny and quiet and barely looked at girls."

"He's changed," Layla muttered. Suddenly, she wanted nothing more than to be at his side. But there were several hundred people separating them.

She and Chelsea allowed themselves to be jostled forward in the direction of lunch. Once they were inside the dining room, guests milled about, finding their spots. A few families, like the Grandins and the Lattimores, had tables for six or eight.

There were multiple two-tops, including the one

where Heath Thurston sat alone at first. But the crowd parted when *Nolan* Thurston strode through the melee as if he owned the place. He shook his brother's hand and sat down.

Behind Layla's shoulder, she heard someone whisper. *I thought those two were estranged. Nolan hasn't lived here in years.*

Chelsea bristled and leaned in to whisper in Layla's ear. "There's our arch enemy Heath Thurston. Have you noticed that *he* hasn't spoken to us? At all? He's letting his lawyers do the dirty work."

"That makes sense," Layla said. "Keeps everything professional and clean. The other guy is the one I told you about who wants to have lunch with us. *Nolan* Thurston. The two Thurstons are twins in case you can't tell."

"Too many of those in this town," Chelsea muttered. "I guess we should sit down."

But Layla noticed that her sister's attention lingered on Nolan.

Layla was just about to cross the room to her table when someone came up behind her and put a hand on her shoulder. "Layla Grandin," the voice boomed. "Hot damn. If I'd known you grew up so beautiful, I'd never have let my brother take my place."

Before she could protest, Jordan Banks whirled her around, hugged her and kissed her square on the lips. Even for a childhood friend, his greeting was a bit much.

She freed herself as quickly as she could. "Hello,

Jordan. How are you?" He did look very much like his brother, but Layla could clearly see the differences.

Jordan shoved his hands in his pockets and rocked back on his heels. "I'm great. Texas-size great. Sorry I couldn't take you to the concert."

"No worries. I had a lovely time with Josh. I guess you and your dad are pretty happy to have him back at the ranch."

Jordan's expression changed visibly. In fact, he looked uncomfortable. That was so unlike him, Layla's stomach flipped. "What did I say?" she asked, trying to make a joke of it and failing miserably.

"I assumed he would have told you," Jordan said. "Joshua has decided he wants Dad and me to buy out his share."

Layla's chest tightened. "Well, he probably hasn't had a chance to say anything," she said, doing her best to pretend this was no big deal. "My grandmother has been ill, and I've been staying with her a lot. This is the first time Josh and I have seen each other in days. Two busy people. You know how it is."

Her scrambled explanation wiped the uncertainty off Jordan's face. Relief tinged his expression. "I'm sure he'll catch you up," he said. "I'd better get to my seat. Dad and I are together today."

"No date?" she asked, wondering if she could make him squirm. Jordan laughed and gave her a naughty grin. "She'll be waiting on me later," he said.

Layla made her way across the room, realizing as she approached her table that Josh had a frown on his face. "Sorry," she said. "Did you think I was never coming?"

"Nah." His smile didn't reach his eyes.

"Are you okay?" she asked, flipping out her napkin and spreading it in her lap.

"Sure," he said. "I see you and Jordan ran into each other."

Her mind raced. Was that pique in his voice? Surely he didn't think Layla had invited the over-the-top greeting or that she was at all interested, despite her old crush. "Your brother can be a bit much," she said. "But yes. We haven't seen each other in at least four years, I think."

The conversation was suspended when the emcee stood at the podium, made a few announcements and then handed out several awards for businesses that had grown substantially in the past year. Finally, the salad course came out.

Thankfully, Josh seemed to shake off his funk. He was funny and charming, and everything a woman could want in a date.

At one point, he grilled her. "You didn't tell your family that you and I were coming to this shindig together, did you? They've all been staring at us for half an hour."

She winced. "Sorry about that. They would have made a fuss. I thought it was easier this way."

"Do I embarrass you, Ms. Grandin?" he asked in a gentle voice.

"Of course not," she said, avoiding his perceptive gaze. "Don't be silly. But I didn't see the point in making a big deal about our date. It's not like we're official or anything."

"Official?" Some of the humor left his face.

"Don't be difficult," she said, lowering her voice. "You know we're just having fun. Who knows what the future will bring?"

"Indeed."

She never knew blue eyes could freeze ice cold. Josh's snarky response lit her temper. *He* was the one making plans to cut himself loose from the ranch where he owned a third of a share, the ranch where he had grown up, the ranch where he had spent many an hour raising hell with his brother and Layla.

The curl of hurt in her stomach grew tighter.

She pushed her uneaten salad away and then had to face the main course.

The pasta primavera was both beautiful and delicious. She poked at it, managing to eat enough bites not to draw attention to herself.

In the end, she focused her unhappiness on the Thurston brothers. "Look at them," she hissed in a low voice. "Sitting there in front of God and everybody as if they're pure as the driven snow."

Josh had been quiet throughout the meal, but unlike Layla, he had cleaned his plate. "They're not criminals. Just because they're claiming oil rights that they think belong to their family doesn't mean they're being vindictive."

"So you're taking their side?" She knew she was being unreasonable, but why wasn't he telling her about his decision not to work on the Bankses' ranch? That was news. Big news.

The dessert course was mostly silent.

Josh had no clue what was going on with Layla. She was upset. That much was clear. He didn't want to think her mood had anything to do with Jordan. Josh had felt sick to his stomach when his brother kissed Layla right on the mouth.

To be fair, Jordan's ebullience was nothing unusual. He was like that with most women. Heck, Josh had seen him hug men and lift them off their feet.

Abruptly, Josh stood. "If you'll excuse me, I need to go to the restroom." He exited the dining room and exhaled. Though the club was well air-conditioned, with that many people in one place, the temperature was rising.

When he came out of the men's room, he nearly bumped into Nolan Thurston. Both of them paused, feeling the awkward moment.

Josh stared at him. "Maybe you and your brother should rethink this oil rights business. The Grandins have a lot of clout in this town."

"Is that a threat, or are you pissed that we're upsetting your girlfriend?"

"If your mother or your sister was entitled to

something—and that's a big *if*—it doesn't follow that the two of you automatically have a claim. Why don't you let this go? Do you have a grudge against Layla's family? Is that it?"

Nolan's gaze narrowed. "What my brother and I are doing is up to us. You wouldn't begin to understand. So I think you should stay out of it. And a word of warning—if you're interested in anything serious with Layla Grandin, you'd better stake a claim. You aren't the only man in Royal to notice her. Things you care about can be taken away in a heartbeat. Be grateful for what you have."

Before Josh could craft a cutting response, Nolan disappeared down the hall.

The man's words lingered, though.

Oddly, Josh didn't think Nolan was a bad guy. But he couldn't figure him out.

Back in the dining room, the luncheon was winding down. People were beginning to leave. He saw Layla with the Lattimore crew.

When Josh joined them, Layla made a general introduction. "I don't know if you all remember Joshua Banks. He moved to Dallas a number of years ago. His dad is Bertram Banks, and Joshua's brother is Jordan."

After a round of handshakes, Layla filled in the gaps. "Jonathan and Jayden Lattimore. Next, their sister and my good friend Alexa, who now lives in Miami, and last, but not least, the baby of the family, Caitlyn."

Josh nodded. Caitlyn's smile was shy, but charming. "Nice to meet you all," he said.

Alexa raised an eyebrow. "I noticed the table for two. Are you the new man in Layla's life?"

Silence fell. Layla's cheeks turned pink. The four Lattimore siblings gave him measured glances as if to say he might not be good enough for their friend. Josh cleared his throat. "Well, I'm a man, and Layla is spending the day with me. As for the rest of it, I guess that remains to be seen."

Layla shot him a look of gratitude and took his arm. "It was great to be with you all today. I'm sure Josh has appreciated the third-degree, so he and I are going to scoot out of here. I'll see you soon."

In the parking lot, they strolled toward the car. He shot his quiet companion a sideways glance. "You up for a drive?"

"I'd love that," Layla said.

He still couldn't pin down her mood. But he was relying on sunshine and speed to smooth any rough edges. It was an impulse on his part to return to the spot where their physical relationship had begun so spectacularly.

When he parked on the exact same hilltop, they got out. Layla's shoes weren't suitable for the rough ground, so she took them off and tossed them in the car.

"Too bad we don't have a quilt," he joked.

Layla's expression was hard to read. "Can I tell you a secret?"

"Sure."

"I spoke with a Realtor this week about buying this property."

"You're kidding."

"Nope."

"But what about the Grandin ranch?"

She shrugged, her expression mutinous. "They don't really need me. Vic is going to take over one day, and if not him, then Chelsea. I've started thinking about…"

"About what?" Josh prompted. He took a strand of hair that had escaped the knot on top of her head and curled it around his finger.

"About having something that's my own. I'm tired of being second-best. Or third or fourth. I'm smart and organized. Nothing says a woman can't own a ranch."

"Of course not." He kissed her nose. "Especially a woman like you."

"So you don't think I'm crazy?"

He saw by her vulnerable expression that she really wanted to know his opinion. "You're a lot of things, Layla, but crazy isn't one of them. You're creative and hardworking. You have everyone's best interests at heart. You're a devoted granddaughter and daughter and sister. I'm damned grateful we reconnected."

Those eyes that kept him up at night darkened. "Me, too," she said softly.

Suddenly, his patience ran out. He cleared his

throat. "Are you still interested in going back to the hotel with me?"

Her gaze widened. "It's the middle of the afternoon."

He kissed her long and hard, pressing her body to his. Feeling the way her fluttery skirt tangled with his pants legs. When he could speak, he rested his forehead against hers. "Do you have a problem with that?"

"No." Her voice was barely a whisper. "Not at all."

Twelve

Layla had a decision to make, and she was running out of time. As Josh sent the car hurtling back toward Royal, she leaned against the headrest and closed her eyes.

She wasn't drowsy this time. Far from it. Her body hummed with sexual energy and anticipation.

Was she really going to sleep with a man—again—who was only interested in having a good time? The truth was brutal. She was halfway in love with Joshua Banks, but she was almost certain he was simply using her for sexual gratification.

Could she handle a physical relationship knowing they were both going to walk away when it was over?

Ever since her conversation with Jordan, she had

waited for Josh to tell her that his dad and brother were buying him out...that he planned to take the money and run.

The question was—run to where?

She knew he had no interest in going back to his ex-wife, but Dallas had been his home for a long time. Surely he would tell Layla if that was what he had in mind. Or maybe he was keeping her in the dark because his plans didn't involve her at all.

Maybe he was enjoying the sex. Maybe she was convenient.

It was all well and good to think about principles and self-respect and doing the right thing.

The truth was, Layla couldn't walk away. He had hypnotized her, enchanted her. That one slender connection—their childhood friendship—had lowered her defenses and let this complicated, devastatingly handsome man walk back into her life with impunity.

From the beginning, he had told her he wasn't sure he was going to stay in Royal. He had admitted that his life was in turmoil...that he needed and wanted to start over. Heck, the man had even confessed to being an emotional mess.

It was her own fault if she had been weaving fantasies about happily-ever-afters with Joshua Banks.

At the hotel, things got real. She knew if she stepped into the elevator with him, the rest of the day was a foregone conclusion. Still, her feet carried her on a path that led to infinite pleasure but an uncertain future.

Josh must have sensed her unease. He took her suitcase from the trunk of the car and handed his keys over to a dark-headed, bright-eyed young man who looked too young to shave, much less park expensive vehicles.

Layla stood on the curb, waiting. Josh joined her and cocked his head, his smile rueful. "This isn't an all-or-nothing deal, sweetheart. I can always take you home."

She searched his face, looking for a sign that she wasn't making a huge mistake. He was kind and sexy and had just enough bad boy in him to make a woman weak in the knees. "I don't want to go home."

It was true. She didn't. *Please don't break my heart, Josh Banks.*

He held her hand on the way upstairs. His palm was warm and slightly rough against hers. She gripped his fingers, telling herself this was light and fun.

But in her heart, she knew. This was Layla putting her heart on the line. Letting herself be vulnerable. Telling the Fates she was ready to try again.

Josh's hotel room was the same. Which meant she couldn't help staring at the bed and remembering the night she had spent here.

She kicked off her shoes and curled her toes in the thick, luxurious carpet. "Do you mind if I freshen up?"

"Help yourself. Then I'll take a turn." He opened the mini fridge and extracted a beer. "We're not in a rush." His teasing smile connected with something deep in her core, setting off a chain reaction of raw need and desperate longing.

Unlike before, it wasn't bedtime. In fact, it was a heck of a long time until lights out. How were they going to fill all those hours?

It was a hot day. At first, she thought about simply using a damp washcloth to remove her makeup and run over her arms and legs. But it seemed dumb to try that when she could simply strip down. She didn't want to get in bed and feel icky.

After the world's quickest shower, she dried off and debated her options. She had imagined Josh removing her fancy dress. But now she didn't want to put it on again. Instead, she grabbed one of the hotel robes on the back of the door, the one that had clearly not been worn.

It swallowed her. She belted it tightly and opened the bathroom door.

Josh looked up, his gaze hooded. Heat flared between them, invisible but undeniable. She thought he would say something. Instead, he brushed by her and entered the bathroom. Moments later, she heard the shower.

His was even shorter than hers. She was still dithering about whether or not to get in bed when he reappeared, wearing the second robe.

A man should look more relaxed, more approachable without his fancy suit. In this case, it was the opposite. Stripped of the traditional clothes he had worn to the luncheon, Josh was even more stunningly masculine.

His damp hair was tousled. Because the robe was belted loosely, a large portion of his beautiful, lightly hair-dusted chest was exposed. His shoulders were so broad, the hotel robe strained to fit them.

Layla found courage and went to him. In her bare feet, the difference in their heights was pronounced. She grabbed the robe's lapels and went up on her tiptoes. "Thank you for being my plus-one today," she said. "Every woman in the room was jealous of me." Then she kissed him.

She took her time, enjoying the taste of his mouth, feeling the intoxicating way their lips clung and parted and pressed close again.

Josh was breathing heavily, his chest rising and falling rapidly. Her own pulse was racketing along at about a thousand beats a minute. So far, he was passive beneath her kiss, mostly letting her take the lead.

She stroked his tongue with hers, growing bolder. He groaned low in his throat. The hair on her arms stood up at the guttural sound.

At last, he gripped her shoulders. "I've wanted you for days, Layla." Was that a note of desperation in his voice? He shed his robe and removed hers. Without warning, he scooped her into his arms and carried her to the bed.

Perhaps he meant to lay her carefully on the mattress, but when Layla bit his bottom lip, his knees buckled, and they tumbled onto the bed together.

Still feeling her power after that sensual, explorative kiss, Layla straddled his waist. "I'd like to be on top. Any objections?"

Josh stared up at her with a narrowed gaze. "Not a single damn one."

Now that she had assumed the position, she was left with a plethora of choices. There were plenty of condoms on the nearby table, but she wanted to play.

Carefully, she stretched out on top of him. She could feel his hard sex against her lower abdomen. Her breasts squished against his powerful chest. Now she could nestle her head on his shoulder and listen to him breathe.

"This is nice," she said primly.

Josh's laughter threatened to tumble her off her comfy perch. "*Nice* wasn't the adjective I had in mind," he said. He cupped her butt in his hands and squeezed. "Interesting. Stimulating. Tormenting. Any of those?"

She put her hands on his shoulders and pushed up so she could see his face. "Sure. I'll take them all. You looked very handsome today. I think I like a man in a suit."

He pinched her ass. "How about a cowboy in dirty boots?"

Awkwardly, she sat all the way up, straddling him. "Do I have to choose? Can't I have both?"

Josh touched her intimately. "If you'll give up this torture, you can have whatever you want."

Without meaning to, Layla closed her eyes. Seeing Josh's hands on her body was too much. Every light in the room was on. What was she doing? She'd never had an exhibitionist bone in her body.

"Josh," she whispered, not even knowing what she wanted to say.

He was a gifted lover. Soon, he had her at the edge of climax, her breath lodged in her throat.

Hazily, she remembered the condoms nearby. "I can't reach them," she said, waving a hand.

"Way ahead of you." The husky words were accompanied by action. He shoved her gently to one side and grabbed a single packet.

When he ripped it open, she stared at him. "Let me do it."

The stain of red on his cheekbones darkened. He handed over the protection. "I said it before. Whatever you want, Layla."

He reclined again and watched her. Her hands shook. This intimacy wasn't one she had initiated very often or at all. During the time she was engaged to Richard, she had been on the pill.

Now when she took Josh's erect shaft in one hand, he shuddered from head to toe. As if she really was torturing him.

His sex was fascinating, long and hard...covered with hot silky skin. She pressed a kiss to the head, eliciting a feral sound from her lover. He grabbed her wrist in one hand. But she ignored his unspoken command.

"Relax," she said softly. "I want to taste you." Taking him in her mouth, she sucked gently, feeling him flex and swell. Feeling the power she had over him was both exhilarating and humbling. But she didn't want power, not really. She wanted a lover who would be her mate, her equal, her partner.

In that instant, she recognized what she hadn't allowed herself to acknowledge. She was not *halfway* in love with Joshua Banks. She had fallen into the deep end—the water over her head. Offering her heart to him madly, passionately, extravagantly.

And yes, he was an enigma. He probably didn't feel the same. Even so, she was helpless to fight the emotion that stung her eyes or to ward off the wave of love and longing that tightened her chest.

"Enough," he said, the word barely audible. "Now, Layla."

She smoothed the condom into place and rose over him, then took him into her body like a silent pledge. This was what she had waited her whole life to find. A man who was worthy of her love.

Soon, she was no longer able to think rationally. Josh filled her completely. Even in the less dominant position, he took control. His hands on her hips might leave bruises. Layla didn't care. His firm hold was the only anchor in her universe.

His gaze locked on hers. "Are you taking what you want, my love?"

She nodded, mute. His beautiful sapphire eyes seemed to be telegraphing a message that was apparently coded in another language, because she couldn't read it. And when he said *my love*, that was just sex talk—right? He couldn't really be as besotted with her as she was with him.

Without warning, he rolled over, taking her with him, never breaking their connection. "Nice trick," she panted.

His low, amused laughter made her blush.

"I don't think I'll let you leave this room," he said, lazily stroking deep.

Layla wrapped her legs around his waist. "We can't screw 24/7."

"Wanna bet?"

She clung to him, feeling the cataclysm build. Josh seemed to know her better than she knew herself. Physically, he met her every need.

When he lost it and pounded hard, head thrown back, cheekbones tight with strain, Layla hit the peak and cried out. It was even better than the last time. Higher. Hotter. More out of control.

Josh came, too, his large frame vibrating. He moaned her name and slumped on top of her. She held him close. Feeling his strength. Memorizing this moment against the day when it might be nothing but a faint recollection.

Like every woman insecure in a budding relationship, she wanted to find the courage to ask where this was leading. But she was afraid of the answers.

Maybe the really brave thing was not to ask at all, but to take what Josh had to give and offer him her heart in return.

He would never know how she felt, perhaps. But a gift was only a gift if it was freely given.

They both dozed for a few minutes.

When Josh finally roused, he yawned. "Wow. You turn me inside out." He was rumpled and heavy eyed and so beautifully male it hurt to look at him.

"Same." She laughed, her heart squeezing.

"We have the rest of the day," he said. "What would you like to do?"

She wrinkled her nose, unwilling to state the obvious.

Josh nuzzled her cheek, kissed the sensitive spot below her ear. "Besides that, naughty woman," he said.

"I'm feeling mellow. You choose."

In the end, it turned out to be a perfect afternoon. They watched a movie in bed with room service snacks. Before dinner, they changed into running gear and did a quick five miles around downtown.

The shared shower afterward turned into something more. Josh took her up against the wall, face-to-face, her arms locked around his neck. It was the most intimately personal thing she had ever done with a partner.

She could swear she saw love and tenderness in his gaze, but the stubborn man never said a word about his ranch share or anything else that mattered.

After dinner in the hotel dining room, they danced to the romantic music of a small orchestra. Layla had packed a full-length red jersey dress that didn't wrinkle. With Josh's warm hand splayed on her bare back, she could have nestled in his arms for hours. But eventually, they went upstairs again.

Josh stared at her when she kicked off her shoes. "Are you happy, Layla?" he asked.

She tensed. "What do you mean?" He might be talking about this day in particular or life in general.

He shrugged. "It's a simple question."

Perhaps this was the opening she had been looking for. Maybe he was waiting for a sign from her. She looked him straight in the eye and smiled wistfully. "Meeting you again has been the happiest thing in my life for a long time, Josh. I have no regrets." That last was to let him off the hook if he was thinking about leaving.

He owed her nothing. No promises had been exchanged, no vows made.

Instead of continuing the conversation, he kicked off his socks and shoes. Then he removed his jacket and shirt and tie. While she watched, he took her wrist and reeled her in, pulling her tightly against his body so they were touching from shoulder to hip. He found the zip at the back of her dress, lowered it and shimmied her dress to the floor.

Now Josh was bare from the waist up, and Layla wore nothing but a strapless black bra and matching panties. "Are *you* happy, Josh?" she asked, her heart in her throat.

He held her tightly, his face buried in the curve of her neck. "You're a very special woman," he said gruffly. "And yes, I'm happy."

She winced. It wasn't exactly the answer she was looking for. When they made love this time, it was markedly different. Less urgency, more tenderness. Was this what goodbye sex felt like?

The question haunted her. She thought for a few moments that she wouldn't be able to have an orgasm, but Josh was endlessly patient. He touched her as if she was infinitely breakable, yet he coaxed fire to the surface. When she finally came, the pleasure was blinding, but tears clogged her throat.

Afterward, they slept, wrapped together in each other's arms. As dawn was breaking, Layla got up to go to the bathroom. When she returned, she climbed back into bed, determined to wring the last drops of pleasure from this interlude.

By the time Josh took her home today, they would have spent the last twenty-four hours together. It felt like forever, but it was far too short, especially since she was no closer than ever to understanding him.

When Josh's alarm went off, they got up and dressed. They both wore jeans and casual shirts. He talked. She answered. But the words were meaningless, utilitarian.

Josh took her suitcase as they made their way downstairs. He kissed the top of her head right before they stepped off the elevator and into the lobby. "This was great," he said. "Thanks for sneaking away a few hours."

"It was fun for me, too," she said. "But I do need to get home and check on Grammy."

Josh stopped suddenly when he saw a trio of men standing on the sidewalk just outside the portico. "I've been trying to get in touch with one of those guys for two weeks." He handed her his wallet. "Would you mind asking for the car? The claim ticket is in there. And give the kid a fifty. He's heading off to college in a couple of months."

Layla nodded. "Of course."

Josh set her suitcase at her feet and jogged over to join the group.

When Layla opened the billfold, she found the claim ticket immediately and passed it to the man at the podium. Then she looked for a fifty-dollar bill.

The money was easy to spot, but as she extracted it, a folded slip of white paper fell out. When she picked it up, her stomach clenched. It was a boarding pass for a flight from Royal to Dallas. Dated the day after Layla first spent the night in Josh's hotel room.

She stared at it blankly, trying to process what she was seeing. Most people had boarding passes on their smartphones now. But in the case of a seat-assignment change or an upgrade, a gate agent might print out a paper boarding pass.

Unfortunately, this was only one leg of the trip. She had no idea when Josh returned.

Why had he gone to Dallas? Why hadn't he mentioned it?

Was this the reason she hadn't heard from him in a string of days while Grammy was recovering at home?

Heartsick and confused, she stood frozen, praying the car would show up soon. The same bright-eyed young man from yesterday handed over the keys. Layla offered the tip. "This is from Mr. Banks," she said, managing a smile.

The boy's eyes widened. "Wow. Thanks."

Layla put her suitcase in the trunk and sat down in the passenger seat. She was numb. Hurt. Stunned.

She must have greeted Josh when he slid behind the wheel. Obviously, they chatted on the way out to the ranch. But she would have been hard-pressed to remember a word.

When Josh pulled up in front of the ranch house, it was all she could do not to bolt up the steps. Instead, she waited while he retrieved her bag. He insisted on carrying it to the front door.

"I'll call you," he said.

"Sure..."

When he bent to kiss her lips, she turned her head at the last minute, making it look casual. Josh's kiss landed on her cheek, not her mouth.

"I'd better get inside," she said, not quite able to meet his searching gaze. "Thanks for going to the luncheon with me."

He frowned, perhaps for the first time realizing

something might be wrong. "I'm glad you asked me. Will you let me know if there is any news about the oil rights?"

"Okay."

"Now that the Thurston twins showed up at the luncheon, I doubt they are going to ride off into the sunset."

She grimaced. "Probably not."

He kissed her again. This one landed smack on her lips—the same traitorous lips that returned the kiss in spite of everything.

Josh pulled back, his expression lighter. "Good-bye, Layla. We'll talk soon."

Thirteen

We'll talk soon. That stupid throwaway phrase rattled around in her head for the remainder of the day. The time to talk was over.

Clearly, Josh's agenda and Layla's were vastly different.

One upside of having a big family living under the same roof was that there were always plenty of distractions. She visited Grammy in her room and was happy to see her looking perky and healthy, even for a woman her age.

After that, she spent a couple of hours in the barn doing her own personal brand of equine therapy. Even though the horses couldn't talk back, Layla told them a few of her secrets. Their soft whinnies and the way they bumped her with their heads eased some of the pain in her heart.

Unfortunately, there was no family dinner that evening. Everybody was either on the run, or like Grammy, eating in their room.

Layla wasn't hungry. She made herself a smoothie with protein powder and forced herself to drink it. At nine thirty, she knew she couldn't procrastinate any longer. Though it was cowardly, she couldn't face Josh. This breakup was happening via text.

Josh...

She typed the single word and stopped, not sure how to say what she wanted to say. He didn't need to know she was in love with him. That would be the ultimate humiliation. Doggedly, she continued.

I know you and I have enjoyed reconnecting after so many years, but my family is in the midst of a cri-sis, as you've heard. Plus, by your own admission, much of your life is up in the air. I think it would be best all the way around if we don't see each other anymore. I wish you every happiness...

Layla

Well, that was it. Short, sweet and to the point. She felt sick. Deliberately torpedoing a relationship that had given her so much joy seemed self-defeating.

But she had no choice. She had too much self-respect to let another man keep her in the dark.

When she hit Send, the tears started. She didn't try to stop them. It was natural to grieve. Joshua Banks was a wonderful man, but he wasn't for her. Clearly, his needs had been sexual, first and foremost.

She hadn't expected a grand gesture. But *something…* Even a generic *I care about you* would have been nice.

Five minutes after she sent the text, her phone rang. If a ringtone could sound angry, she fancied this one did. Of course the caller ID said Josh Banks.

Just this one more conversation and she would be done.

She wiped her face with the back of her hand and answered.

"Hello?"

Josh's voice reverberated with confused rage and maybe even a hint of desperation. "What the hell, Layla? What's going on?"

She swallowed hard. "I think the text was self-explanatory. I've said all I have to say. Goodbye, Josh."

"Wait," he said urgently. "Don't hang up. Did something upset you? Is it your grandmother? Or the Thurston brothers? Let me be there for you."

"It's none of that, Josh. Just what I said in the text. Besides, I don't think you and I have much in common. Please let this go."

Dead silence gripped the phone connection for long seconds.

"You didn't seem to mind our differences when I was giving you multiple orgasms," he said tersely. "Talk to me, Layla. Please."

He was breaking her heart into tiny little pieces. She almost capitulated. But then she reminded herself that Josh Banks was only interested in sex. He had kept Layla on the periphery of his life. She needed to make a clean break.

"Goodbye, Josh."

Heartbreak was a funny thing. Layla was able to function almost normally during the daytime. But the nights were long. And painful.

After spending hours in Josh's bed, it was impossible to pretend that her own lonely room was where she wanted to be. She had done the right thing. No question about it. But oh, how it hurt.

In fact, her intense suffering told her more clearly than ever that Richard had damaged her pride and her self-respect, but he had never really possessed her heart. How had she believed she was in love with him?

It was possible Chelsea sensed something was wrong, but she gave Layla her space. That was a good thing, because Layla was holding herself together by sheer will. Sympathy from her sister would have pushed her over the edge.

In the midst of her grief, she struggled with her

grandmother's secret. And she finally decided that she had to tell her family at least the bare bones of it.

Three evenings after her exchange with Josh, the whole clan was in residence for the noon meal. Grammy had been picked up by a friend whose granddaughter was taking both women to lunch in town.

When the housekeeper had served the main course out on the back veranda, Layla set down her fork. "I have news," she said, keeping her voice low. "Grammy didn't want me to tell any of you, and I promised, but you deserve to hear at least bits of it."

Her father scowled. "My own mother conspiring behind my back?"

Chelsea thumped the table. "Oh, for heaven's sake, Daddy. Don't be so dramatic. Let Layla finish."

Five sets of eyes stared at her with varying degrees of suspicion. Only Morgan smiled. "Go ahead, Layla."

"Because of Grammy's wishes, I can't tell you all the details, but suffice it to say that she came across some of Grandy's scribbles. I've seen them. Unfortunately, it does seem as if Grandy and Augustus Lattimore offered the oil rights to Heath Thurston's mother."

Three beats of silence passed. "Hell," her father said. "I didn't want to hear that."

Vic stood and paced. "What are we going to do?"

Layla exhaled. "I thought we might be morally bound to produce this *thing* Grammy found.

Grammy says not. It's not anything close to being a legal document. Simply a passing reference. The burden of proof is on the Thurston brothers."

Chelsea stood as well, running her hands through her hair. "Good Lord. Are we really going to let them dig up this ranch?"

"We may not have a choice," Layla said. "Still, that photocopy we got from the lawyer has to be substantiated before things go any further."

The housekeeper returned, and all serious conversation was abandoned. But Layla could see from the expressions on everyone's faces that they were all concerned.

She was, too. Of course she was. But her breakup with Josh loomed larger at the moment. Maybe that made her a bad daughter. She didn't want to see her family's ranch ruined. Truly she didn't.

Despite that, Heath Thurston and the contested oil rights were the least of her problems.

When ten days had passed after the spring luncheon at the TCC, her nerves reached a breaking point. No one needed her at the moment. She had to get out of the house, off the ranch.

When she was in her car and driving, one particular spot called to her. She tried not to go. It was pointless to make herself miserable for no reason. But by the time she had traversed all the back roads of Maverick County, she discovered she couldn't return home until she made one final pilgrimage.

The Realtor had never called Layla back. Maybe

she was too busy selling actual houses and ranches to deal with a tract of land out in the middle of nowhere.

Layla made her way to the very same hilltop where she and Josh had first made love. Was that why she wanted to buy the land? Was she trying to preserve that day forever in her memory?

She got out of the car and leaned against the tree. A light breeze made the afternoon heat bearable. Overhead, a buzzard flew in ever-widening circles. Maybe he sensed the death of Layla's love life and was waiting to pick at the bones.

Even in her pain, she had to laugh at her own joke. She wasn't the first woman to want a man she couldn't have. And she wouldn't be the last.

It was just that the moments with Josh had seemed so very *real*. So perfectly intimate. So natural. So right.

The truth was, her romantic judgment still sucked.

She felt the tree bark against her back. Bits of sunlight made their way through the leaves and branches overhead. Time passed. Layla wasn't wearing a watch, and she didn't care. Maybe she had a bit of Irish in her. Perhaps she was holding a wake for the death of her dreams.

Loss was hard any way you looked at it…

Eventually, heavy clouds began to build, and the humidity increased. Texas weather was capricious. A storm was on the way…

She honestly didn't know how long she had been

standing there when she heard an alien noise. Not a bird. Not the wind. Not even an animal.

Instead, as the sound grew closer, it became clear that she had a visitor. When she glanced behind her where the road wound down the low rise, she clenched her fists. How could he possibly have known she was here?

When Joshua parked beside her car and got out, she schooled her face to show indifference, despite the fact that her heart was bouncing all around her rib cage.

"Are you psychic?" she asked with an edge in her voice.

"No. I went out to the ranch. Your sister told me you had gone for a drive. I took a shot." His voice was flat.

Layla didn't move. But she managed to gaze at him without flinching. He looked terrible, frankly. His beautiful hair hadn't been combed. His mouth was set in a grim line.

She went on the attack, hoping he would leave. "What do you want, Josh?"

He leaned against his car, arms folded across his chest. "I think I deserve an answer. Something other than the bullshit you gave me in a text and over the phone. One moment I had a warm woman in my bed, the next she was colder than a witch's tit in December."

"Charming," Layla drawled. "Is that the way men talk to women back in Dallas?"

"Cut the crap, Layla," he said sharply. "Why did you bail on us?"

Temper was better than despair. The hot rush of anger and indignation felt good. "There was no *us*," she said. "*Us* implies a relationship. You saw me as a fuck-buddy."

"Don't be crude," he snapped. "It doesn't suit you."

She infused her voice with ice. "Your opinions are irrelevant."

Suddenly, the aggression in his stance disappeared. For a split second she witnessed uncertainty. And pain? Surely not.

He stared at the ground and then back at her. "I thought we had something special, Layla. I could swear you felt it, too. What happened?"

She'd had enough. The Band-Aids she had slapped over her emotional wounds were being ripped away by this postmortem. "I'll tell you what happened, Joshua Banks. You lied to me, just like my ex-fiancé. You and Richard are cut from the same cloth."

Fury flared in those blue eyes she saw in her dreams. "I *never* lied to you," he shouted. "Never."

Could she jump in her car and drive away? Would he stop her? She honestly didn't know. And if he touched her—at all—she feared she would let him lie to her again.

She took a deep breath, wanting to destroy him with the force of her disappointment. But rational, cooler thoughts prevailed. "Lying by omission is still lying. I get that you weren't sleeping with other women when you were with me. But the end result was the same. I told you I had trust issues with men. You knew my weakness, and you exploited it."

Bewilderment brushed his features. "I honestly don't know what the hell you're talking about. I thought we were getting closer every day."

Either the man was a very good actor, or he thought what he had done wasn't wrong. Probably the latter.

It angered her that she had to spell it out. Because it made her humiliation complete.

"Okay, Josh," she said. "Here it is. You asked your father and brother to buy out your share of the ranch, but you never thought to mention it to me. You flew to Dallas for some unknown reason, and again, I didn't merit even the briefest of explanations." She swallowed, her heart aching. "Those are not the actions of a man involved in a relationship. You're a loner. Or maybe you just don't see me as having any lasting effect on your daily life. Either way, I don't want or need that. I don't want or need you."

Whew. That last sentence was a huge lie. And with the clouds churning overhead, the possibility of a lightning strike was not merely theoretical.

During her big speech, Josh went white. In fact, his pallor was disturbing. Grief and shock turned his eyes dark. "Oh, God, Layla. I—"

Just as he started to speak, a powerful bolt of lightning split a small tree less than three hundred yards away. The thunder was simultaneous.

His face changed. "We've got to get out of here."

Huge drops of rain began to fall. "Goodbye," she said, tears filling her eyes.

Josh took her shoulders in his hands. "I need twenty minutes," he said, his eyes as wild as the sky. "Swear to me you'll listen for twenty minutes."

A second beautiful but deadly lightning strike sizzled the air a little farther away. "Why? It's pointless."

He had to raise his voice to be heard over the wind. "Come to my room at the hotel. We need a quiet place to talk."

"Oh, no," she said, horrified at that idea.

"Please, Layla. You can sit by the door if it will make you feel better. Twenty minutes. That's all I ask."

It began to rain harder. Soon, they would be soaked. "Fine," she said, swallowing the pain of being near him again. Surely she could endure twenty minutes. Then this would all be over.

"We'll go in my car," he said. "I'll send someone for yours later."

"Absolutely not. I'll follow you."

They faced off, Layla resolute, Josh increasingly frustrated. A third lightning strike settled the matter. She dove for her car and locked herself inside. Josh stared at her grimly, got into his own vehicle and then began carefully turning around.

When he started down the hill, she followed him. They had made their decision in the nick of time.

The clouds opened up, and the rain let loose in huge driving sheets. The noise inside the car was deafening. Even with her wipers on high, she could barely see out the front windshield.

It didn't help that the rough lane they had come up was little more than two ruts in the ground. The entire hilltop was turning to mud.

She breathed a sigh of relief when they made it out to the paved road. For a few moments she considered eluding Josh and driving home. Unfortunately, she knew him well enough to assume he would simply follow her.

There was no way in heck she wanted to handle this volatile situation with her family looking on. She wouldn't put it past Josh to enlist their help.

The drive back to town shouldn't have taken more than twenty-five minutes. Today, it was almost twice that. Josh was forced to creep along at fifteen miles an hour. In some places, flash flooding was a definite risk.

Her hands were clenched so tightly on the steering wheel that her neck muscles gave her a headache.

It seemed like an eternity.

Finally, they pulled up beneath the hotel's portico and got out. Though she hadn't gotten drenched, she was wet enough to know she looked bedraggled. She grabbed her purse and joined Josh.

Neither of them spoke in the elevator.

Layla stared at the floor. No matter what he said,

she wouldn't be manipulated. His behavior was clear. He only wanted Layla in bed.

At last, Josh unlocked his hotel room door and stepped aside for her to enter. Immediately, Layla grabbed a desk chair and dragged it to a position right beside the door. Josh's lips tightened, but he didn't respond to her deliberate provocation.

Instead, he went to the bathroom, grabbed two towels and returned, handing one to Layla. She pulled a tiny mirror from her purse and checked her reflection. Not one-hundred-percent drowned rat, but close enough. She ran the towel over her damp hair and then combed it out.

When she was done, Josh sat down on the side of the bed. He looked so defeated and miserable that she almost relented.

She glanced at her watch pointedly. "The clock is ticking."

His spine straightened. He looked at her, an intense gaze that seemed to see inside her soul. "I love you, Layla."

Shock reverberated through her body. And stunned joy. Though it took all she had, she kept her expression impassive. What kind of ploy was this?

"I suppose you forgot to mention that, too?" she said.

He flinched visibly. Perhaps her sarcasm had been over the top, but for him to pretend now made her angry. She wanted so badly to believe him, but she couldn't trust that his words were real.

"I am *so* sorry," he said.

She shrugged. "For what? Things are what they are."

He rested his elbows on his knees, staring at her, coaxing her by the sheer force of his personality to look at him. "This isn't a game. I love you. I suspected it the first time we made love, but I knew it the night you spent in this very room."

Inside, she began to shake. "No."

He stared at her. "Yes. I've lived through what love isn't…which is why I knew so quickly when the real thing hit me hard."

"You don't have to do this, Josh." Her throat hurt from holding back tears of emotion. Everything he was saying delighted her. But was it sincere?

"Layla…" He looked frustrated now. "I know I messed up, but not for the reasons you think."

"What are you trying to say, then?"

Josh shrugged. Unbelievably, his face flushed as if he was embarrassed or bashful or both. What was going on?

He rubbed his jaw. "I was trying to make a grand gesture. All the planning and juggling was falling into place. I was almost ready."

"For what?"

"To make my pitch. To propose."

The joy tried to return, but Layla kept a lid on it. She shook her head slowly, wondering for a moment if this was an odd dream. "You were going to propose to me when you hadn't even said *I love you*?"

He muttered a word she had never heard him use. "I screwed up, okay? I was so busy trying to surprise you that I made you feel shut out and unimportant. That was never my intention."

Now he was definitely embarrassed. She didn't know what to say. Did she believe him? Could she?

When she didn't say anything, Josh doggedly plunged on with his explanations. "The reason your Realtor couldn't find any information about that piece of land you wanted to buy is because my sale was already in progress. I thought you and I could start a ranch of our own. Partners. Lovers."

She was dumbfounded. "You bought a ranch. For us. But you didn't think to include me?"

He stood now and paced. "I was all into this big surprise idea."

"I *hate* surprises," she said.

"Well, I know that now." He went to the mini fridge and grabbed two bottles of water, then tossed her one of them. "Drink something. You're kind of pale."

Layla caught the plastic container automatically. When she opened the lid and took a sip, she realized how thirsty she was. The whole encounter had made her dizzy and uncertain. This wasn't how romance unfolded in rom-coms. She was so tied up in knots, she didn't know *how* to feel.

When she finished two-thirds of the bottle, she sighed. "Go ahead. Finish your story. Tell me about your secretive trip."

He clearly didn't like the adjective, but he didn't quibble. "I went to Dallas twice actually...for a couple of reasons. I met with my ex-boss and pitched him the idea of me working remotely. It's not really a stretch, and I was pretty sure they needed me."

"And did they?"

"Apparently so. He gave me my job back with a raise. I figured if I was going to have a wife and a brand-new business venture, I was probably going to need some income flowing in until the ranch was up and running."

"A wife?" Her stomach quivered. Maybe dreams really did come true.

"A wife," he said firmly.

Layla was giddy, but she wanted the whole story. "You said *two* reasons. What was the other one?"

He stopped by her chair and rubbed the back of his hand over her cheek. His gaze narrowed, those beautiful blue eyes dark with intensity. "Do you love me, Layla?"

She hesitated. She couldn't help it. Trust was hard. She saw that her reaction hurt him.

When she didn't say a word, he crouched beside her. "Don't be afraid of me, Layla. I can't bear it. Don't be afraid of us."

He was so close. So very close. All she wanted was to launch herself into his arms, but this was crazy. Wasn't it?

"We barely know each other," she whispered. She waved a hand. "Give me some space, please." What she wanted him to do was ignore her demand, but then he wouldn't be the honorable guy she loved.

A frown line appeared between his brows, but he went back to his seat on the bed. "We've known each other for years," he said, the words flat. "Lots of people are still close to friends they met in grade school. Our connection may have weakened with time and distance, but once we were together again, I *knew* you."

"But love?"

His jaw was tight. "Men and women come from different planets, right? We look at the world differently."

"What's your point?"

"When you and I were intimate, our bodies connected in more than a superficial way. We saw each other's weaknesses. Our failures. Our hopes for the future. That kind of sex is rare, Layla. Tell me you realize that."

"I haven't had a lot of sex," she admitted. "Except with Richard the rat."

"And was that sex good?"

Fourteen

The room was so quiet, a person could have heard the proverbial pin drop. She thought about it for a moment. "It wasn't *not* good," she said. "Besides, my mother always warned Chelsea, Morgan and me not to ever confuse sex and lust with love. She told us it was a common female mistake."

"Was that what happened with Richard?"

That one stumped her. "Not exactly. I thought he was something I was *supposed* to want. Love and marriage and kids."

"And how did you feel the first time you and I were intimate?"

She thought back to that day. The quilt. The sunshine. The remarkable way she was at ease with Josh and yet so intensely aroused. "I felt like I was flying," she admitted.

At last, a tiny smile of relief tipped up the corners of his mouth, that mouth and those lips she wanted to devour. He watched her closely, so very closely. She didn't know whether to be flattered or worried. And he seemed to be waiting for something more. So she kept talking. "I don't think you know me as well as you think. I'm pretty boring—an introvert for the most part. And I'm not very adventurous. I like tending to the animals at the ranch. It grounds me, makes me feel safe."

He stood again. This time, he took her hands and pulled her to her feet. "And what about me, sweet Layla. Do I make you feel safe?"

It was an odd question, perhaps. And not very sexy according to the rom-com script. But he was so close and so very dear to her.

She took one step and rested her cheek over his heart. "You do," she said. And it was true. No matter how bizarre his behavior, now that he had explained, all her feelings for him came rushing back. She wasn't mad or angry or uncertain.

All she felt at this exact moment was *safe*. And relieved. And if she allowed herself to relax—so very, very happy.

Suddenly, one last question bumped up against her burgeoning peace. She was afraid to ask it. With Josh's big warm body pressed against hers, all she wanted was to bask in the incredulous glow of this man's confession of love.

But the tiniest doubt remained that perhaps he had unresolved issues with his ex.

She swallowed the lump in her throat. "I still haven't heard that second reason you went to Dallas."

Deep in his chest, a groan rumbled. He pulled back, looked in her face and bent his head to kiss her. Tenderly at first, but then with that wild passion that always washed over them and birthed insanity.

"Don't move," Josh said.

She put her fingers to her lips. They tingled. As she watched, Josh rifled in what looked like a piece of carry-on luggage and extracted a turquoise box. When he turned around, his expression was a mix of sheepish defiance.

"A buddy of mine manages the Tiffany store near University Park," he said. "I picked out a ring two days ago and made him swear I could return it if you wanted something else."

Before she could react, he knelt in front of her, tossed aside the outer package and white ribbon and flipped open the real box. "Marry me, Layla," he said, his voice husky. "I adore you. I want to spend the next fifty years making you happy."

He pulled the ring out of its nest and slipped it on the third finger on her left hand.

Somewhere along the way, Layla forgot to breathe. It seemed to be a common problem when Josh was around.

The ring was stunning. A single, flawless, round diamond. At least two carats, maybe more. The platinum setting included a duo of blue baguettes flanking the solitaire.

Josh rubbed his thumb over her knuckles. "Two sapphires," he said. "One for your eyes and one for the wide Texas skies where I found my soul mate."

She tugged him to his feet and searched his face. "Are you sure?"

His gaze was clear and heated. "Absolutely. But you still haven't answered my question. Do you love me, Layla Grandin?"

She sighed happily, holding up her hand to make the ring sparkle. "I definitely do."

Her honesty was rewarded with a world-class kiss. He held her tightly. Enough that she felt the evidence of how much he had missed her pressed against her.

His voice rumbled in her ear. "Will you marry me, Layla? Will you be my wife and my lover and my best friend? Will you build a ranch and a home and a family with me?"

For the first time in her adult life, she was absolutely sure she knew the right answer to a very grown-up question. She pulled back and smiled at him, her eyes brimming with happy tears. "I will, Josh. I will."

Epilogue

Five days later...
Las Vegas, Nevada

Josh held Layla's hand as they stood outside the wedding chapel. Even with dark sunglasses on, he had to squint against the blinding sun. He bent his head so he could see her face. "It's not too late to change your mind, sweetheart. You're a Grandin, the first in your crew to get married. You should be wearing a ten-thousand-dollar dress and having the entire population of Maverick County come out to see society's latest bride in all her finery walk down the aisle."

He worried that she would regret what they were about to do.

Layla removed her own sunglasses and gave him a sweet but naughty smile. She was wearing white, a sexy sundress that bared a lot of skin and show-cased her body. "I don't want that," she said firmly. "In fact, it sounds dreadful. We can always have a fancy reception later. Besides, with this oil rights controversy dragging on, I don't think the timing is right for a big splashy wedding."

It was also why they weren't taking a honeymoon right now, other than two nights in Vegas. Josh kissed her forehead, not wanting to muss her makeup before they tied the knot. "If you're sure. I don't want to upset your family."

She laughed. "I guess that's one benefit of being the forgotten child. No one cares what I do."

He had a hunch she was dead wrong about that one, but he was getting his beautiful bride, so he was willing to be convinced. "Come on, darlin'. Let's do this."

Hours later, Layla couldn't remember a word of the vows she had spoken. Nor the officiant's face, or even the flowers she carried.

But what stood out was Josh's steady gaze and the unmistakable love in his eyes. When he looked at her like that, she knew she had won the jackpot.

At the moment, he was downstairs procuring some kind of surprise. When he told her that a few minutes ago, she had gaped at him and then rolled her eyes.

Josh swore this was one surprise she would be happy to receive.

When a knock sounded at the bedroom door, she checked the peephole and let him in. "That was quick."

Josh grinned. "All I had to do was check at the front desk." He handed her a large white envelope. "Happy wedding day, Ms. Banks."

Layla, definitely puzzled, opened the flap. She'd halfway been expecting another box with jewelry inside. Even when she extracted the sheaf of papers, it took her a second to understand what she was looking at. And then it sank in.

Her heart raced. "I thought we couldn't close until next week." They had added her name to the pending sale several days ago.

Josh kissed her forehead on his way to open the bottle of champagne that was chilling in a bucket on the dresser. "The sellers were eager to be finished. All the paperwork is final. You and I will sign on the dotted line day after tomorrow when we get back to Royal, but the deal is done." He lifted his glass and handed her one. "We own a ranch, Layla. Just the two of us."

Her heart fluttered in her chest. "Do you really think we can do this?"

"Of course we can. It's going to be the best damn ranch in Texas."

She drained her champagne and put her arms around his neck, pressing close, hearing him inhale a sharp breath. "I adore you, Joshua Banks."

He nuzzled her nose. "The feeling is mutual." His

big warm hands settled on her ass. "I like this wedding dress. A lot. But you'll be more comfortable if you take it off."

"Josh…" She ran a fingertip over his lips. "You're so thoughtful."

He shrugged, feigning modesty. "I'll do anything for my sexy bride."

"Anything?" She unbuttoned his shirt.

His face flushed. She had a feeling it *wasn't* the alcohol.

"Anything," he muttered. He picked her up and carried her to the bed. They had both laughed about the candy-apple-red bedspread with the embroidered cupids. Josh flipped back the covers and set her on her feet. Then he undressed her in record time. He took a deep breath and exhaled slowly. "I wish we hadn't wasted so many years."

Layla shook her head slowly. "Not a waste, Josh. Not entirely. We've grown. Pain and heartache do that to a person. But now I *know* what I want. I want you. For better or for worse. I love you."

She kissed him, trying to tell him without words how much joy he had brought to her life. Josh trembled as he held her tightly. Layla trembled, too. They were so lucky to have found each other.

He rested his forehead against hers. "Vegas is all about gambling, but what we did today isn't a risk. Not to me. I've never been surer of anything in my life. You're my one and only, Layla. I love you."

His words healed the scars on her heart.

They scrambled into the bed, and Layla helped with the rest of his clothes. When they were both naked and panting, he went up on one elbow and stroked her hair. "How do you feel about having twins?"

Layla gaped at him. Her heart raced in fear and delirious joy. "Oh my gosh. I never even thought about that."

Josh rolled to his back and laughed so hard tears filled his eyes. "If you could see your face," he gasped.

Happiness filled the room, swirling in the air. Fizzing like the champagne.

Layla stroked his chest, enjoying the buzz of sexual anticipation. She had no doubts. Not a one. This man would be by her side until they were old and gray.

"We did all this so fast I didn't have a chance to get *you* a wedding present," she said, feeling guilty.

Josh pulled her close. Kissed her hard. Settled between her legs, ready to go. His hot gaze stole her breath. "I have everything I could possibly want right here, my love. Now, close your eyes and let's see if we both remember how to fly…"

* * * * *

Don't miss the next book in the
Texas Cattleman's Club: Ranchers and Rivals

Boyfriend Lessons

by Sophia Singh Sasson

#2875 BOYFRIEND LESSONS

Texas Cattleman's Club: Ranchers and Rivals
by Sophia Singh Sasson
Ready to break out of her shell, shy heiress Caitlyn Lattimore needs
the help of handsome businessman Dev Mallik to sharpen her dating
skills. Soon, fake dates lead to steamy nights. But can this burgeoning
relationship survive their complicated histories?

#2876 THE SECRET HEIR RETURNS

Dynasties: DNA Dilemma • by Joss Wood
Secret heir Sutton Marchant has no desire to connect with his birth
family or anyone else. But when he travels to accept his inheritance, he
can't ignore his attraction to innkeeper Lowrie Lewis. Can he put the
past behind him to secure his future?

#2877 ROCKY MOUNTAIN RIVALS

Return to Catamount • by Joanne Rock
Fleur Barclay, his brother's ex, should be off-limits to successful rancher
Drake Alexander, especially since they've always despised one another.
But when Fleur arrives back in their hometown, there's a spark neither
can ignore, no matter how much they try...

#2878 A GAME BETWEEN FRIENDS

Locketts of Tuxedo Park • by Yahrah St. John
After learning he'll never play again, football star Xavier Lockett finds
solace in the arms of singer Porscha Childs, until a misunderstanding
tears them apart. When they meet again, the heat is still there. But they
might lose each other once more if they can't resolve their mistakes...

#2879 MILLION-DOLLAR CONSEQUENCES

The Dunn Brothers • by Jessica Lemmon
Actor Isaac Dunn needs a date to avoid scandal, and his agent's sister,
Meghan Squire, is perfect. But pretending leads to one real night...
and a baby on the way. Will this convenient arrangement withstand the
consequences—and the sparks—between them?

#2880 CORNER OFFICE CONFESSIONS

The Kane Heirs • by Cynthia St. Aubin
To oust his twin brother from the family company, CEO Samuel Kane
sets him up to break the company's cardinal rule—no workplace
relationships. But it's *Samuel* who finds himself tempted when
Arlie Banks awakes a passion that could cost him everything...

Focused on finishing an upcoming album, sound engineer Teagan Woodson and guitarist Maxton McCoy struggle to keep things professional as their attraction grows. But agreeing to "just a fling" may lead to everything around them falling apart...

Read on for a sneak peek at
After Hours Temptation
by Kianna Alexander.

Maxton eyed Teagan and asked, "Isn't there something I didn't get to see?"

She smiled. "If you mean my bedroom, you gotta earn it, playboy."

"Sounds like a challenge," he quipped.

She shook her head. "No. More of a requirement."

He laughed, then gently dragged the tip of his index finger along her jawline. "You're going to make me work for this. I just know it."

Her answer was a sultry smile. "We'll just have to see what happens."

"Truth is, I really don't have the time for a relationship right now."

If she took offense at his statement, she didn't show it. "Neither do I."

"So, what are we doing here?"

She shrugged. "A fling? A dalliance? I don't think it really matters what we call it, so long as we both understand what it is…and what it isn't."

Their gazes met and held, and the sparkle of mischief in her eyes threatened to do him in. "Enlighten me, Teagan. What will we be doing, exactly?"

"We hang out…have a little fun. No strings, no commitments. And, above all, we don't let this thing interfere with our work or our lives." She pressed her open palm against his chest. "That is, if you think you can handle it."

"Seems reasonable." *I like this approach. Seems like we're on one accord.*

Her smile deepened. "Tomorrow is my only other free day for a while. Why don't you meet me at the Creamery, right near Piedmont Park? Say around seven?"

"I'll be there." He wanted to kiss her but couldn't read her thoughts on the matter. So he grazed his fingertip over her soft glossy lips instead.

"See you then," she whispered.

Satisfied, he opened the front door and stepped out into the afternoon sunshine.

Don't miss what happens next in…
After Hours Temptation
by Kianna Alexander.

Available June 2022 wherever
Harlequin Desire books and ebooks are sold.

Harlequin.com

Love Harlequin romance?

DISCOVER.

Be the first to find out about promotions,
news and exclusive content!

Facebook.com/HarlequinBooks

Twitter.com/HarlequinBooks

Instagram.com/HarlequinBooks

Pinterest.com/HarlequinBooks

YouTube.com/HarlequinBooks

ReaderService.com

EXPLORE.

Sign up for the Harlequin e-newsletter and
download a free book from any series at
TryHarlequin.com

CONNECT.

Join our Harlequin community to
share your thoughts and connect
with other romance readers!
Facebook.com/groups/HarlequinConnection

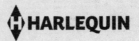